BAD BOYS DO IT *Better*

5

In Love With an Outlaw

A NOVEL BY

PORSCHA STERLING

DEDICATION

This one is dedicated to my readers. Thank you for asking for a part five! Now that I've written it, I don't know how I could have possibly wanted to end the series without it. It was very necessary. I appreciate you!

Previously...

*T*he crisp smell of jasmine blew in the air as birds chirped their witness of how beautiful a day it was. The sun was high, but there was a gentle breeze that provided relief to all the guests as they flowed into the chapel. Inside the chapel, Kane stood with his thick brows knotted in worry as he looked around the packed church, wondering if the crowd could see the thoughts racing through his mind.

"She's not coming," he said, before letting out a short burst of air. It felt like it was all he had left in his lungs. "She's not... I know it."

"She is," Cree assured him, but his face did not follow his words. His lips were pulled into a straight line and his brows were bunched together, like was natural for someone who was struggling to make their mouth say something their mind didn't believe.

"Don't sweat it, fam. She's coming," Luke affirmed once again. "She's just late. It's only been twenty minutes. I should kick her ass for bein' on CP time tho."

"She late as hell, but she's comin'," Yolo added. Tank walked up with a chicken bone in his mouth. Obviously, he'd already taken it upon himself to dip into the reception food before the ceremony had even gotten a chance to start.

"Stop actin' crazy, nigga. You know Teema is comin'. Calm da fuck down," he voiced in between chomping on the chicken wing.

Kane shook his head, pushing away his brothers' words the

instant they said them.

"No… she's not late. That's not like her. She's never late for shit."

"Yo, if this is what it's like to be married, I'on know if I want that shit," Luke said, cutting his eyes at Kane. "Got niggas actin' like a bitch and shit."

Before Kane could respond with the fist he'd balled up by his side, the doors of the church opened and everyone turned towards the sound. The sunlight burst in, temporarily blinding Kane from seeing whom it was standing before him. But then his eyes adjusted and his heart filled with a joyous feeling that he never knew he could feel. She was there.

There at the front of the church stood Teema, dressed like an angel. Her hair fell in loose curls around her shoulders and a hibiscus flower hung near her ear. She was the perfect picture of beauty, style, and grace. Everything that he needed in his life. His heart swelled in his chest as he stared at the only woman who had his heart. The one he would love to vow his life to… forever.

"She purrrrty," Luke teased, jabbing Kane in the side.

Cree, Yolo, and Tank nodded in agreement, each of them happy for their brother, but thinking about their own women: Cree was thinking about Carmella, Yolo was thinking about Sidney, and Tank… Tank was thinking about a woman that he'd just started to date—wasn't sure where it would go, but he felt like he wanted to make it official. After feeling the guilt that hadn't yet left him after Faviola's suicide, he vowed that he would change his love life for the better and start acting like the grown ass man he was. The new woman in his life demanded that after all.

"I now pronounce you husband and wife," Janelle said, looking from Kane to Teema, who hadn't taken their eyes off each other for the entire ceremony. "You may kiss the bride."

When Kane grabbed his new wife and pulled her into a deep embrace, Luke took the opportunity to grab Janelle and kiss her as well.

"Luke!" she gasped, smacking him on the shoulder once he'd let her go. "That is sooo inappropriate! This is *not* our wedding!"

"It could've been but you playin' around with a nigga heart," was Luke's only reply. He smiled at the disgusted look on Janelle's face, completely unfazed by her response.

One of these days she'll realize who the hell she's dealing with, he thought to himself before blowing her a kiss and reaching out to rub her round belly. She smacked his hand away but all it made him do was laugh. Every single day of their lives, she made him the happiest man on Earth.

In the past few months, Janelle hadn't changed her mind about getting married before her career took off, but Luke knew it was coming soon. The week after she told him they had a baby on the way, he bought her a multi-million dollar estate that made the place she'd grown up in look like a shack used to house slaves. True to his style, he was not to be outdone by any muthafucka when it came to Janelle— and that included her father.

After initially refusing to move in with him, Janelle gave in as soon as she laid eyes on the house. Luke had spared no expense, and it was obvious he'd picked the house with her in mind. She had an office so that she could work from home, a nursery that rivaled something put together for a celebrity's seed, and many other rooms specifically decorated just for her to enjoy—even a room specifically for her to watch *Scandal* in with photos of Olivia Pope all over the walls, along with some of her most famous sayings: 'It's handled' being Janelle's favorite.

The more Janelle thought about it, she was already living the life of Mrs. Murray…all that was left was to make it official. She hadn't told Luke yet, but she already had a date in mind for the wedding and was now determined to make sure they tied the knot before their baby girl was born.

As Teema and Kane walked out of the chapel, hand in hand, the groomsmen and bridesmaids walked down behind them. Cree and Carmella smiled at each other before grabbing each other's hands. Cree tucked Carmella's body in close to him and felt a flutter in his chest that he had been feeling more often than not when he looked at her and they locked eyes.

She's the one.

The past few days those three words had been cycling through his mind and he knew it was true. He knew that Carmella was the one, and he knew that he needed to follow after his brothers Outlaw and Kane and put a ring on her finger. But the stubborn side of him couldn't see asking Carmella to be his so soon. Unlike his brothers, Cree wasn't the one to take the plunge so fast and preferred to date Carmella just a little bit longer before locking her down. It wasn't just because of the man he was; it was also because of the woman she was. She loved her freedom just about as much as she loved him. He knew that it wasn't the time to lock her down.

On the good side, she was attending school in New York instead of Los Angeles, a decision she'd made on her own so that she could be close to him. What she didn't know is that whether she transferred schools or not, they would have been together because if she hadn't, he had been prepared and ready to move to Cali in order to be with her.

At the reception, Teema tossed the bouquet with a certain lady's name in mind, and that same woman was the one who caught it. Sidney hadn't even been really trying to participate and was only even standing in the vicinity of the bouquet toss because of Carmella's urgings, but when the flowers landed right inside of her open palms, she couldn't help but smile and cut her eyes at Yolo, who was staring at her with a love-struck expression on his face. No love was perfect and theirs was definitely anything but that, but it was true, it was honest, and it was forever.

Tank fingered the newest charm that he wore at the end of his gold link chain. It was the letter 'F' for Faviola and every time he looked at it, he was reminded of her and the promise that he made to himself that he would never play with a woman's emotions in the way that he'd played with hers. Truth be told, Tank did feel like he loved Faviola, and he felt like he could have settled down with her, but his need to always have more than what he needed became a curse that was hard to shake. And, eventually, yielding to those selfish desires cost him when Faviola decided to take her own life.

Tank had been minding his own business at Janelle's office

warming party when he met a woman who stole his interest in a way none other ever had before. It wasn't just the fact that she was beautiful—although she was—and it wasn't the fact that she was smart—even though she was incredibly intelligent, too—but it was the fact that she had a spark about her that resonated deep within him the moment they locked eyes.

Tank didn't even know that Mixie was Janelle's sister; he had no idea how they even knew each other or why she'd been invited to the party, but he made up in his mind that he *would* ask her out, and he *would* be a good man to her if she gave him the chance to be. The good news was that she did give him the chance and he'd been working at being a better man every day since. They'd only been official for a couple months so far, but Tank had to say that he was really enjoying riding the 'one woman only' train along with his brothers. Maybe being in love was all people claimed it to be.

"Get your big belly ass over here, Janelle!" Luke yelled, earning a frown from Janelle before she walked towards him with her mouth poked out. "The hell you trying to catch the damn bouquet for? I done put a muthafuckin' ring on yo' finger already and dropped a baby in yo' gut, but you still don't wanna marry a nigga. You don't deserve the bouquet or none of that other shit I done gave you. Go sit'cho big stomach ass down!"

If Janelle had been a few shades lighter, her cheeks would have shown ruby red from embarrassment. Everyone nearby howled in laughter at his words, but she only grunted and turned her nose in the air as she walked in the opposite direction. *Waddled* in the opposite direction was more like it, seeing as she was eight months pregnant but really looked like she was around twenty months.

"I'm just playin' wit' yo' ass. Stop takin' shit so serious," Luke apologized, grabbing her by the hand. He pulled hard, tugging her just enough so that she turned in his direction.

"You forgive me?"

It was hard for Janelle to stop the smile from cracking through on her lips when she saw the pouty face that accompanied his question. No matter what he did, she would always love this man and would always forgive him.

"No, I don't," she replied, but Luke knew the truth.

"When you gon' marry me though? For real?" he asked her with all seriousness in his tone.

For some reason, her wearing his ring wasn't enough. Even the fact that she lived in the house he'd bought for her and was about to have his baby wasn't enough. He wanted Janelle to have his last name. He wanted to feel like she was really his. He felt like his greatest accomplishment in life would be the moment she became his wife. It was crazy to him how the woman he thought he would hate when he first laid eyes on her in the courtroom, was the woman that he couldn't see himself living without.

"Luke..." Janelle started, her words dying off as she wondered if she should go ahead and tell him what she'd been thinking. She wanted it to be a surprise, but she should have known that wouldn't work well with Luke. When it came to him, things rarely went according to plan.

"I decided that I want to get married before the baby comes..."

It was all Janelle had to say. Bending down, Luke held her tightly in his arms and kissed her like he didn't know they weren't the only ones in the room. He was actually well aware that they weren't, he just couldn't bring himself to care.

"The way you just tongued a nigga down got me second-guessing if I really wanna get my golds put back in," Luke teased once they broke their embrace. "You gon' still kiss a nigga like that if I do?"

Janelle grimaced her disgust. "Ew, no. I won't be kissing you with that yuck mouth."

"Yo' ass was doin' a lot more than kissin' this yuck mouth back in the day," Luke reminded her with a cocky smile.

He walked away to chill with his brothers for a little while, leaving Janelle thinking back to the very beginning of when they met. It was insane to her whenever she thought about how they became the couple they were. Back then when she was Janelle Alexandria Elizabeth-Ann Pickney, the oldest of four girls, graduate of New York Law School, two years earlier than expected, at the top of her class and the apple of her father's eye, no one could ever have convinced her she would fall in love with one of the most dangerous men in all of New York City.

"I guess that's why they say 'we make plans and God laughs,'" she muttered under her breath as she shook her head and took one last look at her man, and husband to be, turning up with his brothers. They had red cups in the air and, from the looks of it, Cree was rolling up a fresh blunt for them to puff on the balcony. Janelle snickered to herself when Luke caught her eye and seductively licked out his tongue at her before walking outside behind the other Murrays.

She had planned every step of her entire life, but never would she have thought she would fall in love with an Outlaw... until she did.

Luke

"*L*isten, fam, I feel in my heart that right now… you *might* be actin' like a bitch."

"Man, fuck you, Outlaw!" Kane waved his middle finger at me right before tossing one of the brown leather cushions from the sofa over his head into the air. With my lip curled, I watched as he reached down and searched all through the seat, pulling out wrappers, coins and everything other than what he was looking for. The nigga was concentrating so damn hard that his face was literally drenched in sweat and he was breathing like a fat boy doing a half-mile on a treadmill. All of this over some dumb ass ring.

"C'mon, nigga, I ain't got time to be waitin' on you." I gave a swift, annoyed kick at one of the sofa cushions that had fallen near my foot during his tirade and checked the face of the watch on my wrist. I had things to do and figured I'd get Kane to roll out with me, but his ass was on some other shit.

"Outlaw, just wait for when you get married, yo' ass will understand this shit. If I leave out this house without my damn ring on and Teema catch me, it's gon' be all kinds of bullshit. Shit been sweet since her mama dragged her ass outta here and I don't wanna get nothin' started. Watch when it's your turn. You'll see."

Lip still curled, I looked at him like he'd forgotten who the hell he was talking to. In fact, I knew damn well he'd forgotten. Dragging my hand sharply across the front of my neck as if telling him to 'cut it out,' I decided to go ahead and set the record straight since he was confused.

"Naw, that ain't gon' be me, bruh. Janelle already know who run this shit and it's *me*, nigga! *She* don't tell *me* what to do. I'm a *real* nigga and real niggas don't follow behind no bi—Oh, shit, hold on, bruh. This her calling me right now."

Bending my head to grab my phone, I could hear the sound of Kane's snickers as I answered my cell and simultaneously shot him my middle finger. Yeah, I was jumping to answer the phone but I had a good reason. Janelle was pregnant with my baby girl and, from the looks of it, she was about a million weeks along. Her ass could drop any day at any given time, and the last thing I wanted to do was miss her bringing my baby girl into this world.

"Yo! What's up, bae?" I put the phone on speaker and smirked at Kane, eager to tell Janelle what his ass was over here stressing about. "I'm over here with Kane and he on some gay shit right—"

"Nigga, don't 'yo' me!" Janelle snapped before I could even get the rest of my sentence out.

Aw, shit.

She was on one.

And I didn't have the slightest idea as to why she was tripping because she was perfectly fine when I left the house, giving her a firm smack on the ass with a nice squeeze to follow before leaving out the door. She'd replied by giggling like a nerdy schoolgirl, complete with a snort, and telling me that I needed to hurry home that evening. Now she sounded like she wanted to kill my ass…usin' the 'n-word' and shit like she was bad. And for what? I ain't know.

Her mood swings had me thrown. I couldn't understand how niggas like Tank managed to keep getting chicks pregnant over and over again because this was my first one, and after going through all this, a nigga was done. I thought that a baby was supposed to calm Janelle down—make her appreciate a nigga for blessing her with my seed—but it had managed to do the exact opposite. Every damn second of every day she was snapping on me about some shit… *Crazy* shit. Then if I bossed up on her ass, she would start pouting and crying like I'd put my hands on her, screaming about how words hurt too.

Waking up in the morning, I never knew what version of Janelle I was gonna get. She was the most beautiful angel with a devilish streak. Some days a nigga was scared to eat the food she cooked, thinking that she was trying to poison my ass because she was acting too nice, and the next day she was liable to throw the food right in my damn face. Every day was like walking through a minefield. I didn't know how to deal with her, definitely didn't want to anger or stress her while she was carrying my seed, so I found myself away more than home, hoping that everything would be better if I gave her some space.

"What's wrong this time, Nell? Damn, I ain't been gone thirty minutes! How could I have done somethin' wrong already?"

"Luke, you ate my shit!"

Giving the phone a vicious screw-face, I squinted at it, totally lost as to what was going on. The hell was she talking about?

11

"Huh?"

"'Huh' means your greedy ass can hear! You ate the food I had leftover from dinner at the restaurant the other day. Why the hell would you do that when you know I specifically saved it so that I could eat it for lunch today? I'm working on a case and I don't have time to stop and walk my big, fat ass somewhere to pick up lunch, and you know I'm sick and tired of take-out so—"

Pressing my fingers to my temple, I let out a sharp breath. Janelle always had a slick ass mouth and pregnancy didn't do nothing but make it slicker. I promise, the day that she twerked my baby girl out, I was slipping the doctor an extra few racks to sew everything down there up so she couldn't get pregnant again.

"Nell, you ate that shit yourself, ma. Last night... you don't remember? You was eatin' it when I got back home from Cree's."

"What?" she half-whispered and then paused, obviously thinking back to the night before. "I ate it?"

Shoulders slumping, I sighed, leaned back on the wall behind me and shook my head. "Yeah, yo' ass was stuffin' ya face when I came in the house. Talkin' 'bout how you was still hungry afterwards. That's why I went to sleep early because I knew you was about to try to run me to the store for some food. I knew that lil' leftover food wasn't gon' last until today when you asked them to box it up. That pregnancy got yo' mind fucked up, ma."

As soon as the words left my mouth, I knew I had messed up again, but it was too late. Like nails in a coffin that had my pathetic ass stuffed inside, my fate was sealed.

"Don't be blamin' *shit* on my baby, Luke! My pregnancy is a blessing and you need to recognize that. Really, the more I think about this, the more I realize that this is your damn fault!"

My brows squished together and my eyes fell into a tight squint. My thoughts quickly ran over the details of our conversation, searching for clarity. Now she had my mind blown. How the hell was I to blame for this?

"Huh? How you figure that shit?"

"Because if you knew the food wasn't going to last until today, you should have ordered me another full plate to go!"

I cocked my head up before shaking it from side-to-side.

Man, she was on some bogus shit.

Holding the phone loosely in my hand, I just about zoned out while she continued getting on my ass about how I was the reason her and the baby would starve today and how I should've been more thoughtful… that if she gotta carry the baby, the least I could do was make sure her basic needs were met. She really knew how to make a nigga feel like shit.

By the time she hung the phone up on me, Kane was standing in front of me with a wide stance, a jutted chin, his arms crossed, and a big ass grin on his face. There were plenty of times and instances that I had to eat my words when it came to fuckin' with Kane, but never before had karma chased me down quite so fast. Stuffing my hands in my pockets, I looked him back boldly in the eyes, tongue-in-cheek as I waited for whatever bullshit I knew he was about to say.

With a slight shake of his head, he licked his lips one time and then opened his mouth to let me have it.

"Listen, fam," he started, flattening his hand against his chest, over his heart, with a faux sympathetic twinkle in his eyes. "I feel in my heart that right now... you might be actin' like a bitch."

***

"Aye, double-check that order for me, lil' mama, if you don't mind. I need to make sure that shit is right."

The baby-faced girl working the counter licked her lips slowly while leaning in close, letting me know that the pussy was up for grabs, before softly nudging the bag of food in my direction. She was the three Bs—brown-skinned, bowlegged, and bad as hell. Janelle needed to thank God every night that I loved her because, otherwise, I'd be fucking ole girl in the back while customers were waiting in line to place their order. But naw... here I was being faithful for once in my life.

Can you believe that shit?

To be honest, I loved Janelle, but it almost didn't seem right to be a single man in the world and turn down all the pussy that was offered to me on the daily. Especially these days when a nigga was hard-pressed to get some from his own chick. Since Janelle's belly grew to cup-holder status, she let it be known that the pussy was officially off limits, telling me that it was hard for her to feel comfortable. When it came to making the kid, I used to have her legs in a vice-grip, pulled back damn near behind her neck, folding her up like a pretzel, and now that she was pregnant, I couldn't do shit. What whack ass part of the game was that?

The chick in front of me sucked her teeth gently, to bring back my attention, before running her tongue slowly along her top row of teeth.

"No need for me to check it, Daddy. I made sure that everything was right for you."

Her hand grazed over mine as she pulled away and I bent my head, chuckling a little at how easy all this shit was for me. Even easier now that I couldn't do a thing about it. She was gorgeous, I couldn't deny it. And it seemed like a slight against the God who created her for me to not give her the attention she deserved, but I had a girl. And this wasn't Janelle.

"Aye, that's what's up. 'Preciate you lookin' out," I replied, grabbing the bag and tossing her the same smirk that was responsible for a lot of panties dropping back in my better days.

"Any time, baby."

Turning to walk away, I stopped abruptly when I nearly ran dead into Kane's big ass who was standing right behind me with a wide-eyed, spooky expression on his face.

"What?"

"You need to be careful, nigga. You finally seem to be on some grown man shit… got your life together. Don't let these thotty thots out here mess it up for you."

Sidestepping him, I bumped his shoulder as I walked by, heading out the door. Kane was always trying to school my ass and today, I wasn't here for the lessons.

"You just worry about Teema fuckin' you up for missin' curfew tonight, nigga. When Janelle first met me, I was the type of nigga who did *what* the fuck I wanted, *when* the fuck I wanted, and that ain't changin'. I put that ring on her finger to lock her ass down but ain't no vice versa come with that shit. She ain't got no lock and key on me."

Jumping in the whip the same way that Kane needed to jump out of my damn business, I waited for him to follow before starting the engine and taking off towards Janelle's job. In the middle of all the things that I had planned for the day, here I was dropping her off some lunch like the good nigga I was. Would I be appreciated for it? Probably not.

"Be right back," I said once I pulled in front of Janelle's building.

Lips twisted to one side, Kane nodded his head and pulled out his phone, probably to check in and tell Teema where he was. It was crazy to me how much his ass had changed since being married. Not only was he trying to pull out of the jobs that I was lining up, but it seemed like the nigga had lost his backbone. Teema ran *all* his shit, and he let her. He was on some 'happy wife, happy life' shit, and I just wasn't feeling it for my situation.

I strutted into Janelle's office like it was my shit, because that's how I walked into any building, but I couldn't help but feel proud of her for the moves she was making. After only a few months of really being in business, she was holding her own. Not counting herself, she had three other first year attorneys, two chicks and one ugly ass nigga, on her team, and all they did was grind. I wasn't too happy about her hiring the dude, but he seemed corny as hell to me so I let it slide. He looked like the type to wear plaid pants and cross his legs at the knees.

After fucking around with a real nigga like me, there was no way that Janelle would fall victim to that feminine shit.

"Hey, Outlaw!"

Dipping my neck, I nodded to acknowledge Sidney who was sitting at her desk, the receptionist desk, in front of Janelle's office. She'd been working here for about two weeks after Janelle fired the last chick, claiming that she was 'too smiley' when I came around. Sidney's grin deepened the closer I got and my thoughts went to Yolo, wondering how things were going with the two of them since they'd finally stopped hiding around and really made things official.

"What's good, Sid?" She shrugged nonchalantly in response and I lifted one brow. "My brother ain't fuckin' up, is he? You know all you gotta do is let me know, and I'll beat that nigga's soft ass right in front of you so you know it's real. Let you get some licks in, too."

She giggled, shaking her head from side-to-side, making her long hair sway behind her. She had performed the biggest magic trick known to man because who would've thought that she had all this sexy shit hidden underneath her Jordan shirts, basketball shorts and sneakers?

"No need for all that. He's treating me just right." Questioning her declaration, I cocked my head to the side and she threw her hands in the air. "I mean it. No complaints over here. He's good, I promise."

"Finally," I muttered and then looked up, noting that Janelle wasn't in her office. "Where that big belly, fat booty chick you work for at? Her crazy ass cussed me out about some food this morning so I brought her lunch."

Sidney snorted out a laugh at my expense and nodded her head knowingly. Frowning, I shot her a greasy look and she cut her chuckles short, but her smirk remained.

"Janelle just walked into the conference room with Gerald. Let me call her for you."

Raking a single finger over my top lip, an effort to stall my rising temper, I nodded my head and waited while Sidney phoned the conference room to let Janelle know I was in the building. A few seconds later, the door to the conference room opened and out walked Janelle holding a stack of folders, giggling and shit with gay ass Gerald by her side. The nigga looked like a white ass, preppy, fraternity boy living in a stuck-up Black nerdy ass man's body. His clothes were tight as hell. There had to be a law against a nigga wearing clothes that muthafuckin' tight.

Tensing up, I tried to hide my disdain at seeing how happy and animated she was talking to this nigga when, these days, it was hard for me to even get a smile out of her. Everything I said or did seemed to piss her off, but from the current look on her face, whatever was coming out of Gerald's mouth was the best thing she'd heard in all her life. She was eatin' up that nigga's every word the same way she had gobbled up that muthafuckin' food she'd accused me of eating.

"Gerald, you wrong for that! Why would you do that girl like that? It's obvious she has a crush on you. Don't lead her on!" Janelle all but gushed, not even acknowledging my presence even though she was standing right in my face.

"Nah, I'm not leading her on. I'm just friendly."

"That's ya gotdamn problem right there. Ya ass too fuckin' friendly," I interrupted, unable to hold my peace any longer and stand by while Janelle played me for a fool. "And what the fuck so damn funny, Nell? Yo' mouth spread wide as shit."

Eyes bulging out of her skull, Janelle finally looked at me, a look of sheer horror and embarrassment on her face. But I wasn't worried about her feelings at the moment, because if she didn't want me to step to the nigga, she shouldn't have been trying me in public like a sucker. It was obvious that she was getting too used to me being all lovey-dovey with her ass all the damn time. She'd forgotten that, at heart, I would always be the muthafuckin' Outlaw.

"Luke! I—"

"No, you're good, Janelle. I got this," Gerald said, placing his hand on Janelle's shoulder, and I felt myself get even more heated. Instinctively, I reached down to my side for my gun and cursed under my breath when I realized it was not there. Lucky for Gerald, or else they'd be carrying his ass out on a stretcher.

Fuck.

Janelle was always complaining about me carrying my guns around all the time and, for some stupid ass reason, I started to listen just to make her happy. It had been a while since I had to bust a shot at a nigga, so I felt at ease with doing as she asked unless I was in the streets. Now I was regretting that shit, and it was time to put the ax to that. No longer would I be walking around without being strapped up, because I was starting to see that niggas were starting to feel comfortable with trying me.

"I'm sorry if I've done anything to anger you, Luke. Janelle and I were working on a case in the conference room when I asked for her advice on a personal issue—"

Licking my lips, I raised my hand to silence him and shook my head. "Listen, bruh, ain't shit personal need to be happening between you and my lady. Keep that shit business, aight? And the name is Outlaw."

Just like the bitch I knew he was, Gerald looked at Janelle before answering me with a nod of his head.

"Yes, sir."

What nigga you know look at a bitch for permission before he speaks? I couldn't take these new breed niggas seriously. They would forever be lame.

"And, on some real nigga shit, keep your hands to your damn self before I snatch them muthafuckas off. You lucky I ain't got my piece on me… for real, yo."

Pushing his lips into a straight line, Gerald ain't say nothing in response, even though I could tell the chump had a lot that he wanted to say. But who the hell cares about what a nigga got swirling around in his big ass head? He knew better than to say shit and that's all that mattered. Without looking towards Janelle, he kept his head straight ahead and walked away to his office, leaving me standing in front of my fiancée, who was glaring right into my face like she wanted to kill me.

"UGH!" Janelle groaned and then stormed off to her own office, slamming the door behind her.

It instantly got under my skin. When my parents used to fight, my pops would always say 'there was nothing like the fury of a Black woman'. Until Janelle, I didn't give a shit about any woman's 'fury' so I was never affected by it. But when she acted like this, it pissed me off so much that I felt like jacking her pregnant ass up on the wall just to teach her a lesson.

The entire building was silent. Looking at everyone, they seemed to be focused on their own business—staring intently at their computers, cell phones, or a stack of papers—but it was a certainty that they'd been ear hustling and heard every damn thing that had just went on. Everybody but Sidney, that is, because her nosey ass was staring dead in my face with her eyes wide; not from shock, because I've known her long enough for her to have seen me snap more than a few times.

"Damn, nigga! I thought you was turning over a new leaf!"

"Fuck that," was what I said in response and snatched the bag of food off the counter before walking to Janelle's office.

I tried the door, hoping that she knew better than to lock it. The way I was feeling, I would have knocked the whole damn door down if she continued to try me. It was niggas like Gerald who would get locked out and go run somewhere to pout about it. Niggas like me would take the shit right off the hinges. The door was unlocked and I felt slightly satisfied that she wasn't about to make me turn into the wrecking crew in this bitch.

As soon as I walked in her office, she pounced on me like a lioness does its prey. Her rage showed in her eyes, as she barreled towards me, baring her teeth.

"I can't believe you did that! This is my place of business, Luke. Gerald is a *colleague*!"

"No, his ass is a muthafuckin' worker who got out of line, but I pushed that nigga back in his place since you wasn't tryin' to do it."

Janelle walked behind her desk and stood there, with her arms crossed on top of her big ass stomach, looking as stubborn as ever. I couldn't even believe I had to explain this simple shit to her—she knew the type of nigga I was. She'd been with me during my craziest of times… she'd seen the stuff I was capable of.

Yeah, I was a lot calmer now since I'd fought to have her in my life, but she was starting to get that shit twisted, mistaking my calm for being soft like her boy, Gerald. I was still the same nigga who demanded and commanded respect wherever I went, and if I felt I wasn't getting it, some shit was liable to get started. Terrorizing the streets until my name had become a constant on the evening news had earned me that respect and fear—it seemed like a few people needed a reminder.

"Don't come at me sideways with that bullshit, Nell," I began, my voice low but the steely nature of it letting her know that I was on the precipice of anger. To anyone who really knew me, they would understand that it was really time to squash all issues because this was the calm that came right before I spazzed. Even though she was mad, Janelle recognized that and her arms dropped to her side to appear less confrontational.

"Every time I come home, I gotta deal with yo' shit. You always nagging a nigga about somethin'. You won't even let a nigga *sniff* the pussy, even though I go above and beyond to make sure you straight.

Then, I drag my ass out here to bring you lunch after you was ready to lynch my ass 'bout some shit that wasn't even my fault, and I see you showing all yo' muthafuckin' teeth to that gay ass nigga, cheesin' and shit all up in his damn face."

Sighing, Janelle dropped her head and I knew she was about to wave the white flag. Even though she'd been acting like a mental patient for the past few months, she had to know she was going overboard with it. And I'd been more than patient with her—thanks to my niggas who was doing all they could to keep me in line. For real, she was really lucky I had my brothers around, because the love I had for her was starting not to be as important as having some peace of mind.

In the past, no matter what drama I set off in the streets, I knew if I went home, I could block out all that shit until I was ready to deal with it. Imagine spending all day dealing with more bullshit than a little bit and then coming home to even more of it. I couldn't even fuck nothing to take my mind off it because she wasn't having that either. I was about a week away from tossing my pride to the side and beating my dick at night to take some of the pressure off, and even the mere thought of that just seemed sad as hell.

"You're right. I know I've been on edge lately, but it's because—"

Before she could finish what she was saying, there was a knock on the door and I turned around. Imagine the look on my fuckin' face when I saw Gerald standing at the door holding a tray of food in his hands, looking like a butler with his nose up high in the air. From my peripheral, I saw Janelle doing some quick motion with her hands as if she were either doing a mime dance, performing sign language or trying to swat a fly. I knew she was most likely trying to warn this nigga to get lost, but it was too late.

"What da fuck you want?!" Gritting on him, I snatched the door open and Gerald got to stuttering.

"I—I—I had ordered us lunch for the meeting and she forgot it in the—"

Reaching out, I slapped the food straight out of his hands, making him flinch when the contents hit him in the chest, some landing in his face. With his expression pulled just as tight as the clown suit he was wearing, he stood stiffly in place with his lips forming a straight line. I could tell he couldn't stand my ass but, like the lame he was, he didn't say a single word.

The glass walls vibrated when I slammed the door, leaving him standing on the other side. Curiosity flared from the outside and I noticed that we had become the center of attention for everyone around us but having an audience never stopped me. With my focus renewed on Janelle, I cocked my head to the side and indignantly pressed my index finger into my chest.

"Does this nigga not know who the fuck I am?!"

The look on Janelle's face was almost pleading in nature. She knew that I was about to snap and she was on the verge of panic. She shook her head profusely, tears brimming in the corners of her eyes.

Here she goes with this emotional shit, I thought.

"He—he's not from here, Luke. Just give him a break, he's a good guy but—"

"Hell to the *fuck* naw." My whole body went stiff and I seemed to go cold when I realized she was really about to stand in my face and defend another nigga.

Tossing the bag of cold ass food onto her desk, I turned around and walked out of her office, slamming the door behind me. If she wanted to run her mouth about that dick-in-the-booty-ass nigga, she could do it on her own time.

Janelle

"He's not home yet?"

Sighing, I gave a downtrodden glance to the clock before standing up to check outside my window for the millionth time, even though I already knew what I'd see once I looked out there. My heart felt heavy.

"No… he's not."

"Damn, he must *really* be mad."

Carmella was definitely not lying. Luke must have *really* been mad. Like for real. In all the time that I'd been with him, he'd never stayed out all night like this. And ever since learning that I was pregnant, he'd never ignored my calls—not even when he was pissed off about something. But this time, not only was he not answering my calls— the nigga had actually turned his phone completely off. When I called, it went straight to voicemail. Thinking that maybe he'd just blocked my number to piss me off, I called Carmella and asked her to dial his number for me to see what happened. The result was the same… her call went directly to voicemail. Luke was really in his feelings.

"I need a favor, Carm," I began with a tone that meant I was about to ask for something that I really wanted but already knew she probably wouldn't want to do.

"Nuh uh, nope! I am not asking Cree about this. Every time you start actin' like a bitch and he gets mad, you call me to see if Cree can smooth things over for you. Not this time; you need to deal with your own problems!"

Pouting, I flopped down on the couch, pulling my cashmere blanket over my bare legs. My stomach was twisted up in knots. There was no way that I could get in my bed and go to sleep peacefully until Luke made it home.

"But how you gon' call me a bitch?"

Sucking her teeth, I could almost see Carmella rolling her eyes on the other end before she replied.

"I said you're actin' like a bitch and we both know it's true. You stay clickin' on that nigga and then wanna call me cryin' afterwards. What the hell is going on with you, Jani?"

I sifted through my thoughts for a good excuse for how I'd been acting lately and came up empty. I really couldn't say shit because Carmella was right, and I knew it. The sad part of it was, I also knew how I was acting was wrong but I couldn't stop it once I got started. A few months ago, no one could tell me that I wasn't the happiest that I'd ever been, because I was. I was engaged to the man I loved and had a baby on the way, things were straight between my dad and me, and my law firm was starting to actually make some serious moves.

But all of that happiness I felt came to an end about a month ago.

A little over two months ago, Gerald started working with me and along with him, he brought one of my biggest clients, Wellington & Co. For the first time since my business was started, I was able to pay my own bills without asking Luke for help and could even bring home a small profit. My dreams were finally becoming a reality at the very moment that I'd started to lose hope, thinking that I was stupid for thinking I could run a law firm on my own and would end up being a jobless housewife.

And I know what you're thinking because I was thinking it, too.

Not Janelle Alexandria Elizabeth-Ann Pickney! A *house*wife? The two things together didn't even sound right, but that's what was happening. I'd sacrificed my goals and ambitions for the sake of love. And maybe to some other woman, it was the ultimate dream to have no responsibilities, no ambitions and simply be the wife of a paid nigga, but to me, that was a complete nightmare.

So my luck changed when Gerald came about, being that he'd interned with Wellington & Co. and was able to convince them to come on as a client. But about a month ago, Wellington & Co. decided that they wanted to pull out after discovering that I was the owner of the law firm Gerald worked at, and finding out about Luke's criminal history and reputation as the infamous menace of New York.

Losing Wellington & Co. was only the first domino to drop. That same week, I lost three more of my clients for the same reason. Of course they didn't come right out and say that it was because of Luke, but I could read between the lines. For clients who had previously been satisfied with my services to all of a sudden claim that they had to terminate our business relationship due to a 'conflict of interest' was an obvious sign.

In addition to failing in my professional life, two weeks ago I received an email from some random email address that I couldn't trace. There were no words, but attached to it was a grainy, distorted cell phone sex video of some man, who resembled Luke, and a woman. I couldn't really tell it was Luke at first, but a few seconds in his voice came through and I knew it was definitely him. Closing the video, I kept the email but didn't finish the video and never looked at it again. I didn't bring it up to Luke either.

The date it was taken was from around the time Luke and I had just started messing around so I couldn't be all that mad because technically he hadn't cheated on me. But seeing the video, even just the small piece I'd looked at, bothered me all the same. Since then, every time he touched me, it came to mind and severely fucked up my mood.

Lately, I'd started being stingy with having sex with Luke because between feeling nauseous and fat all the time, it was uncomfortable. But even though that was all true, it wasn't the only reason. No matter how much I tried to push it from my mind, I couldn't stop thinking about how somewhere out there, some bitch had a video of her and Luke having sex and was using it to fuck with me.

And, baby, believe me when I tell you that the pressure of holding in all this shit had my ass going insane! Some days it felt like I had steam coming out of my ears and was about to boil over. I knew that the way I was treating Luke was my own passive aggressive way of punishing him for doing things that weren't his fault—he couldn't help that I was losing out on clients because of the reputation he'd earned way before me. And the video happened before we were a couple so I couldn't fault him for doing the things a single man was supposed to do.

Still, at the same time, I couldn't help the rage that took over whenever I thought about what I was losing out on by being with him.

His life remained perfectly intact while my shit was collapsing all around me like a tower made of cards. I was pregnant well before the age I'd planned on having children, my career was taking a nosedive, driving me crazy as I tried to hide it and I was single-handedly destroying my relationship by pushing away the man I loved, simply because another woman had found a way to virtually push my buttons.

Still holding the phone to my ear, I rubbed the back of my neck with my other hand, trying to relieve some pressure.

"I'm just stressed," I said to Carmella finally. "Maybe it's the hormones getting to me."

The piece of me that hated to admit defeat couldn't even tell my sister about what was going on in my life. I grew tense at the thought of telling her that I'd worked my whole life towards a goal that I was so close to obtaining but now had to let slip away because I was a fool for love.

"Well, you need to take a bubble bath, massage, or something to get a handle on it. Whatever it is you need to do to calm your ass down so you can stop going in on your nigga every damn day... do it!"

"But if you could just ask Cree—"

"I'm not asking Cree shit," Carmella dismissed me roughly, true to her selfish nature, having little regard for my state of distress. "Besides, we've got our own issues."

She let out her last words along with a giant puff of hot air, making me wonder what could possibly be going on with the two of them. Last I'd heard, everything was peaches and cream—Carmella was in school and Cree was supporting her while she followed her dreams. And by support, I meant that he was spoiling her with all the bells and whistles that came with living the high life as girlfriend to a paid nigga. Besides staying in the books, Carmella stayed in the stores shopping about as much as she also stayed in the club.

"What issues do y'all have?"

"This may sound stupid but I don't want judgement, okay?" Lifting my brow, I stopped myself from reminding Carmella that she'd done more than enough dumb things in her past for me to pass judgement on.

"Promise. What is it?"

She expelled air and then there was a pregnant pause.

"Well?" I pushed.

"You ever felt like things were going too well? Cree and I aren't really having any issues and it's making me feel…" She paused, trying to collect her thoughts into the right words.

"Like you may be overlooking something in your relationship?" I assisted her. "Everything is just right and you're waiting for the drama that is definitely on the way?"

"Yes!" Carmella's voice pierced through my eardrum so forcefully that I had to pull the phone away. "That's exactly how I feel."

Shaking my head, I replied, "Carm, you do this all the time… in every relationship, you eventually go looking for drama. Why can't you accept that you deserve to be happy?"

There was another pause and then Carmella's voice came through, much lower and more somber in tone than before. "Because every time

I've gone looking in the past, I've found something that snatches away my happiness. Men *always* disappoint."

To hear Carmella sound that doubtful about being happy in love saddened me.

"Just because you've experienced bad things with men in the past doesn't mean that's what you'll get with Cree. He's very different from anyone you've ever been with," I reminded her and she snorted as she forced out a tense chuckle.

"You can say that again."

Before I could inquire further about her personal business, I heard a key enter the lock in the front door and I nearly jumped straight up in the air—a remarkable feat being that I was eight months pregnant and had been lying flat on my back.

"Carm, let me call you later!" I blurted out before quickly hanging up the phone.

My heart thrummed within me and my thoughts ran rampant with things that I should say as soon as I saw him. The door swung open and Luke swaggered in, sexy as ever, instantly making me feel stupid about everything that had happened between us earlier. When I thought on everything we'd been through since the day we decided to be together, it really wasn't worth it to be fighting over stupid shit.

My breath stalled in my chest when Luke's fiery eyes rose to meet mine, widening a bit in surprise at seeing me standing across from him. Exhaling softly, he stood in place and ducked his head before running one hand through his hair, which was loose in a messy but sexy halo that hung down far below his shoulders. He pulled his black hoodie over his head and his shirt lifted with it, exposing his washboard abs before he had a chance to adjust it. My lady lips began to throb in response and I squeezed my thighs together in an attempt to control my desire.

"Luke... I'm sorry. For everything."

Pensively cradling his chin between his thumb and the side of his index finger, he kept his eyes low for a minute, averting away from my stare. I could see the thoughts running through his mind even though I had no idea what he was actually thinking. That simple fact had my emotions on edge.

"Baby, please. Just forgive me. I—I don't wanna fight anymore."

Luke still said nothing and made no movements to indicate that he even heard me. The silence around us was so suffocating to me that I could barely breathe. I was at a loss for words to say that I thought could fix our situation, so I bit down on my bottom lip and decided not to say anything at all. He needed space and I was going to give him that for now, and hopefully... *hopefully* we could set everything straight between us in the morning.

With my shoulders slumped over in defeat, I began to walk to our bedroom and was almost there when I heard his heavy steps echoing behind mine. In the next instant, his hand was on my forearm, gripping me hard before he pulled me back, fully knocking me off balance. I stumbled backwards into him and he cradled me lovingly in his arms, hugging me gently from behind.

Tears sprouted in the corners of my eyes as I relaxed into him. He pressed his lips to my temple and kissed me so softly that, for a second, I wondered if I'd imagined it until he roughly whipped my body around, gripped my chin firmly with his hand, and crushed his lips against mine, kissing me like the roughneck I knew him to be.

His hand probed all of the curves of my body, rubbing and caressing me while sucking hungrily on my lips and sampling every bit of my mouth with an eager tongue. When he forced my thighs apart and inserted his fingers into my soft spot, I felt my knees go weak. This was the man I fell in love with; the one I'd recklessly risked it all for, throwing caution to the wind. How I could spend so much time pushing him away, I didn't know.

Without breaking our kiss, Luke lifted me up with ease, as if I didn't weigh nearly an extra thirty pounds, and laid me gently across the bed. Then he separated his lips from mine, leaving me no time to mourn their departure before placing his head between my legs. I felt his breath gliding across the sensitive skin of my clit and I squeezed my eyes shut in sweet anticipation.

The second his tongue pushed through to my center, I gasped and nearly came on the spot. He worked me like a pro, exploring every bit of my folds like he'd designed them himself. He knew exactly what moves set my body on fire and in less than a few minutes, I was thrashing and crying out for mercy, gripping his soft hair in my hands as he lapped eagerly between my thighs. Though I begged him to stop, Luke only went deeper, bringing more intensity to my already Earth-shattering orgasm.

"Daaaamn, baby!" I was positive I couldn't take anymore but Luke's nature was to consistently push the limits. Reaching down, I tried to push him away but he clamped his lips around my nub, sucking hard as I struggled not to lose my mind.

"Stop running from me."

He released me from his grip and I was able to somewhat catch my breath. When I opened my eyes, I was pleased to see him holding his long, thick rod in his hand, stroking it gently while staring at me like a starved animal, even though I'd already given him a good meal. Once again aroused, I licked my lips in craving. I wanted nothing more than to feel him inside of me.

Like a genie, he granted my wish and entered me slowly, easing in with caution as if he didn't want to hurt me. Shifting my hips, I opened wide and pushed against him, forcing him to slide in a little faster. My lips parted and my head fell back when he'd filled me completely and started stroking me, long and hard, bringing me quickly to the brink of another climax.

He grabbed my nipples, squeezing hard as he slammed into me. I clenched my teeth together, loving the feel of his hard body against mine. His lips brushed across my neck and then he began sucking and kissing as he rocked his hips into mine, making love to me in the sweetest way. A low growl escaped through his lips before he hoisted my thighs up with his strong hands and started thrusting into me with sharper strokes, still at a steady pace and not too fast, but with more vigor, grinding into me hard like he was trying to merge our flesh into one.

Trembling subtly, I sucked in a breath and rode the waves he was stirring up through my middle, until I was on the brink of another orgasm. I parted my lips to speak; I wanted to beg him not to stop but I was so overcome with how I felt. Luke began to work into me a little faster and I knew that he was approaching his climax. A cold breeze blew over my body and my skin prickled. Nearing my moment, I gnashed my teeth together and then went stiff as a board. I came for the second time at the same exact moment that Luke released into me, breathing heavily, his eyes closed while he enjoyed the moment.

"Pregnant pussy really is the best pussy," he enthused with a grin while looking down at me. I rolled my eyes and but couldn't stop the edges of my lips from turning up into a smile.

"Yo' lil' evil good pussy havin' ass." He slapped me on my thigh and then stood up and walked to the bathroom. As light-hearted as it had sounded, I knew what he'd said was only a half joke. I had been acting evil and I needed to get myself together before I messed around and lost my man.

Seconds later, Luke casually whisked out of the bathroom holding a Heineken he'd stashed in some hiding spot I knew nothing about and laid on the bed next to me with his white tank pulled back behind his neck, showing off his washboard abs. Although seeing him that way was always so sexy to me, I felt my stomach suddenly begin to churn when my thoughts went back to the sex tape. My eyes filled with tears and before I knew it, one escaped and slid down my cheek. Sniffing, I wiped it away quickly and turned away so that I wasn't facing him.

"You okay?"

"Yeah."

No sooner than the lie had left my lips, Luke had pulled me onto my back, jumped on top of me, straddling me between his thighs, and pinned my arms to the bed by my wrists. The sparkle in his eyes told me that, although he was being playful, it wasn't all just fun and games. He was suspicious and he wasn't going to back down until I came clean.

"You're lying." Cocking his head to the side, his eyes narrowed in on my damp cheek. "Nigga, what you cryin' for?"

My eyes shot to away from his face and my thoughts merged momentarily. I felt childish about what I was about to ask him but I knew I had to anyways. When women gushed about how wonderful it was to be pregnant, no one ever touched on the insecurities that came along with it. No one ever spoke about how hard it was to watch your expanding waistline and wonder if your man's attraction to you ever changed.

No one ever spoke about how it was hard to keep yourself from asking yourself if he was disgusted by the way you looked, wobbling around like Humpty Dumpty the egg, with dry ass hair, dry ass skin, and acne that you thought you'd left in your early teenage years. And, then there was this stupid sex tape which reminded me of Luke's overactive sex life before me... did he wish he could go back to those days and, once again, experience the high men got from jumping into new pussy each day? Was I enough?

"Are you happy with me?" I almost whispered. "I mean... with me being pregnant and all. Am I still beautiful to you?"

A blank stare settled in his eyes and I held my breath in anticipation of what he would say. Biting down on my bottom lip, I shifted my eyes to his navel and watched the rise and fall of his breaths.

"Get the fuck out of here, Nell. You for real?" he asked and then lifted my head up by my chin. "Look at me... you serious?"

More tears came as I nodded my head shamefully, mashing my lips together to keep from crying. Luke made a scoffing noise and shook his head, his messy mane of a ponytail shaking slightly behind it.

"I want you to listen to me... not *hear* me, I need you to *listen*," he started, leaning down close to my face so that he could have my full attention. "There is no woman on this Earth who is more beautiful to me than you are right now. Yeah, I know I joke around, saying shit about your fat ass belly, but that's all it is. A *joke*. You're the woman I love more than I love my damn self. And you're carrying my child... ain't shit anybody can do to make me want them more than you."

Relief flooded through my veins, sending chills all throughout my body. I nodded my head and wiped at my damp eyes, sniffling my tears away. Luke gazed at me for a few seconds longer before bending down towards my shoulder, as if he were about to go for a kiss, and sinking his teeth into my skin, clamping down just hard enough to make me wince.

"Ow! What did you do that for?" I knotted my brows together and rubbed my throbbing shoulder.

"Because I hate that shit... don't ever doubt yourself when it comes to me, Nell. What kind of man am I if I can't show you where you stand with me? If you feel like another bitch got somethin' on you, what does that say about how I've been doing with makin' you understand how much I love you and how beautiful you are?"

Eyes narrowed and pinned on mine, he waited for me to respond, but I could only shrug. I'd never looked at it that way. Luke had never given me a reason to feel insecure. I could honestly say there was no reason for me to feel threatened by another woman. Maybe I needed to take the same advice I'd given to Carmella and stop looking for something wrong when there was nothing.

"I guess it's the... hormones," I replied and offered him a weak smile.

His frown broke and he smirked before rolling off of me and grabbing his Heineken from off the nightstand next to him.

"Just like you said earlier... don't be blamin' shit on my baby girl. This one ain't on her; all this is just you. You better straighten that shit out before I put yo' ass in time out. Make you thug it out in the guest room with that lil' ass sheet you got on the bed in there."

He was insane, right? I couldn't be the only one to think that. Even so, I had to admit that I couldn't live without him in my life.

Carmella

*H*ave you ever been with a nigga who didn't do a damn thing outside of what he was supposed to? One who was faithful, honest, and always did exactly what he said he was going to do?

Yeah… me either. Not until I got with Cree anyways.

It was crazy how drama-free my life was at the moment. *Unbelievably* crazy. Especially for someone like Cree who was a man in his late twenties, sexy as hell, and fully on top of his shit. In addition to that, he was a Murray and every woman under 50 who knew about the Murray brothers wanted to get with one. He was getting tossed pussy left and right in front of my face so I knew them heffas ain't have no manners behind my back. Something was going on and I knew it. There was no way that Cree had cut off all his hoes so quickly once I entered the picture. But I also knew one other thing… whatever he had going on, I was going to find it.

"Baby girl, what are you tryin' to do?" Bryan asked, walking up behind me as I searched through Cree's Macbook. He never left it at home when he went out, but I'd caught him slipping today and I just knew he was hiding something on it. Why else would he make sure it stayed locked and in his sights at all times?

"I know that this nigga is up to something and I'm about to find out what it is. His sneaky ass is not about to play me for a fool."

Smacking his lips together, Bryan sighed heavily and walked around to sit in the chair in front of me. He crossed his legs at the knee and tilted his head to the side, sizing me up like I'd gone crazy.

"So let me get this straight... you're with Cree and you feel since everything has been going perfectly for the past few months that he just *has* to be cheating on you?"

Okay. Hearing Bryan say it quite like that sounded ridiculous. I'll admit that much.

"It's a woman's intuition, Bry. Like..." I paused, letting my eyes lift to the sky as I thought about the best way to explain what I was thinking. "Like you ever just felt like you didn't *deserve* for things to be going as great as they are? That something had to be going wrong?"

Sitting up straight, Bryan looked at me with bug eyes. "Hell no, bitch. I'm *fabulous!* I ain't never felt no dumb shit like that! Listen, Carm, you are tripping. Close that man's computer and let's get the hell out of here. There are some sales I wanna hit up before we go out tonight."

Frowning stubbornly, I shook my head. I knew I was right about Cree hiding something, but I couldn't explain why so I took Bryan's advice and shut down Cree's computer. I was placing it back in Cree's hiding spot when I heard the front door open and slam closed. Just as I was able to scurry away from it, Cree stormed into our bedroom with a deep frown on his face, his eyes searching around the room.

"Back already?" I asked Cree. His eyes rose and widened a little as he looked from me to Bryan, almost as if he was just realizing that we were there.

"Yeah, I forgot something. Hey Bryan, what's up?"

"Nothing much, boss," Bryan replied from where he was sitting at my desk, his legs crossed and his hands politely folded over his knee.

"What did you forget? You want me to help you look for it?" I asked like I didn't already know exactly what he was looking for.

"Naw, I got it." Bending down, Cree grabbed his computer from where I'd just placed it and I couldn't help but roll my eyes. Bryan turned to look at me and I gave him a pointed look. Cree was crazy about that computer and I knew it was for a reason.

Before pushing the computer inside of his bag, Cree paused, frowning hard as he looked down at it in his hands.

"You been on this?" he asked, holding it up, his eyes searching mine.

"Huh? No… why?" Cree's focus stayed on me and I began to feel antsy, knowing that he'd always been able to pick up on my lies in the past. Hopefully, I'd become a little better at hiding things than I had before.

"It feels warm but I haven't turned it on since last night," he explained and I licked my dry lips, trying my hardest to keep my cool. "You sure you ain't been on it?" His eyes narrowed into mine and I knew I was about to crack. I swear, I couldn't lie to save my life.

Sensing that I needed to take a different approach, I sucked my teeth and rolled my eyes. One thing that Cree couldn't deal with was my attitude. It threw him off his game every time because he hated confrontations.

"Cree, what the hell you questioning me about that for? You got something on there you trying to hide? Like, damn! Why I gotta lie about using your computer?"

Cree paused for a few seconds, staring at me hard before he blew out a breath and shook his head. When I saw him push the computer into his bag, I let out the breath I'd been holding and relaxed slightly.

"Yo, chill. I was just askin' a question."

"Well, the answer is no," I emphasized with my arms crossed.

"Yeah, I know. I'll be back later on, okay? It might be late but not too late."

He turned to leave and I stood up, walking behind him. "You aren't going to tell me where you're going and when you'll be back?"

Without stopping, Cree looked over his shoulder and glanced at me. "No, I'm not goin' to tell you where I'm goin' because it ain't none of your business. And I already told you when I'd be back."

I started to object once again, but I could tell from the look in Cree's eyes that I wouldn't get anywhere by doing so. When he decided to shut me down, he shut me all the way down and no matter how much I pouted, complained, and yelled about it, he wouldn't budge.

Feeling hopeless, I stood in the hallway and watched as Cree walked down the hall without bothering to turn around and look at me or even give me a kiss goodbye. When the front door opened and closed, I was still standing in the same spot but Bryan had walked up behind me. I let out a long sigh before turning around and looking into his face. He wore a contemplative expression with his lips twisted up to the side and his arms crossed in front of his chest.

"Okay… I might have doubted you earlier but not anymore. That nigga is definitely hiding something and, between the two of us, we are going to find out exactly what it is."

***

I lived for my weekends with Bryan. Wherever he went, shit was live and I was happy to be in the mix. I thought that my partying days were far behind me once I stopped using coke to get things popping, but Bryan quickly reminded me that there was no need to use anything to turn up… we could get things started on our own. And he was definitely right.

"I need to sit my ass down!" I squealed, grabbing onto Bryan's forearm as he ushered me off the dancefloor. "I don't think I've ever danced this much in my life!"

Bryan cut his eyes at me and jerked his neck to the side to give me a look over. "Bitch, no, you haven't. I thought your ass was about to break a sweat and that's why I snatched you up. Ain't shit cute about getting hot and sweaty in the club."

Smiling, I rolled my eyes but continued to walk to the bar with Bryan, pretending like I didn't see every man in the club nearly break his neck to look in my direction. I wasn't showing off my body anymore on Instagram, but that didn't mean that I stepped out the house looking like a nun. Wearing a short bodycon dress with the highest heels you could buy out the store, I knew that I was easily the sexiest thing in the room. I'd recently received my new lacefront in the mail and was sporting it, giving me a look that could only be rivaled by Beyoncé… maybe.

Going out with Bryan every weekend gave me a title that I hadn't even been seeking when I first started, but earned from taking pictures of all the crazy shit that we did when we were out and then posting them on my Instagram page. I was Carmella the socialite, and instead of people checking my page for my body, they were checking it to see what club or party was the place to be. In fact, I'd gathered up such a name for myself that some clubs were even paying me to show up and post pictures of all the fun we had while there. Blogs were using my pictures and asking me to rate the places where I partied so they could use the material to write reviews.

They could call me a lot of things, but one thing they couldn't call me was broke. Even though Cree was paid, I always found a way to earn my own money by doing the things I loved.

"Now that we're sitting down, let's talk about what is going on with you and these niggas you been dancing up on." Bryan finished his statement by keeping his eyes pinned on me as he sipped brown liquor out of his glass with his pinky stretched to the sky like it was tea.

"Nothing to talk about. I'm just having fun," I replied with a smirk and a slight shrug. "Nothing wrong with dancing. And it makes for good pics for my page."

Bryan huffed out a heavy breath. "Nothing wrong with it as long as your nigga ain't crazy. Don't mess around and get both of our asses beat. Cree is working with a loose cannon. He's quiet, but that nigga ain't got it all when it comes to your pretty ass."

Rolling my eyes, I grabbed the glass in front of me and paused a little before sipping. "Wait… what is this?"

"Just drink the damn drink, Carm! Ain't no alcohol in it. I told Jerome to give me the liquor and you the juice. Don't worry."

Although there was nothing wrong with me drinking, I knew it usually got me in trouble so, unless Cree was with me, I avoided alcohol. With a sigh, I swiveled around in my chair to look at the crowd and started sipping while bobbing my head to the music. After spending the entire week cooped up in the house studying my ass off so that I could get my GPA up, it felt good to be out of the cage. Cree was a homebody at heart and it was rare that he wanted to do anything that involved leaving the house after whatever it was he did in the streets all day.

Two girls who were definitely white-girl wasted stumbled over in front of me, using each other for support as they wobbled in their stilettos and asked if they could take a picture with me. With a grin, I grabbed both of their phones and took a series of photos, some smiling, some with my tongue out, and one with me chucking the deuces with a mean face like I was throwing up gang signs.

"Thank you so much! Carmella, we *love* you!" One of the girls shrieked before running forward with her arms wide to give me a hug. She fell into me and I grabbed her, helping her from busting her ass as I hugged her back.

"And I love you too, doll. Now go have fun but not too much fun, okay?" I told her as I pulled back and stared into her eyes. Her lips formed a smile and she nodded her head sincerely before staggering backwards to join her friend.

"That bitch is wasted."

"Naw, that bitch is high," I corrected as I watched the duo stumble away, dancing offbeat. Shaking my head, I wondered if I'd ever looked that fucked up in the club when I was getting high. It was disgusting to see and I never wanted to go back there.

"Hurry up and drink that lil' apple juice you nursing," Bryan told me before looking at the face of the diamond crusted watch on his wrist. "The night is young but we got about three other spots we need to hit before turning in. You've got a full night tonight, honey."

"Yes, manager," I joked and rolled my eyes before downing the rest of my drink.

Grabbing my phone, I checked it to see if Cree had called or texted but, as usual, there was nothing. I wasn't surprised. On more than one occasion, Cree had shown me that he didn't approve of my club hopping on the weekends, but he knew he couldn't say shit about it. At the end of the day, I was making my own money and I wasn't showing my ass to get it, so what was it for him to complain about it?

"This place new?" I asked, strolling into the last club of the night. It was well after 3 am but I wasn't the least bit tired.

Eyes scanning the room, I took in the luxurious details with admiration, making a mental note to include it all when I gave my opinion on the place later on. It had a lounge vibe, with large white leather sectionals sprawled out over the room, but the dancefloor was large and packed nearly to capacity because the DJ was on point. Walking in, I couldn't help bopping a little to the beat.

"No, not new, but it's got a new owner who is well-connected so celebrities frequent his spot. I'm not sure why he's paying for publicity from you because he sure don't need it. Just last week, Rihanna was here and, now you fly… but, bitch, you damn sure ain't no Rihanna!"

Cutting my eyes to Bryan, I was about to check him but ended up joining in with him in laughter. He was right, I wasn't no Rihanna but I was getting paid to frequent the same places she did so, all in all, I considered myself a winner.

"I'm going to the bar. You want me to order you something?"

Nodding my head, I pulled out my phone. "Yeah, go 'head. I'm going to take a few flicks right quick and then I'll be over there."

Turning my camera to take selfies, I moved back onto the dancefloor and pressed the button to make a quick video for Snapchat before going live on Instagram. While winding my body to the beat, I kept the camera high to capture the ambiance, the club décor and, of course, me as I put on for the camera, keeping it extra sexy.

"Heyyyy lovebugs!" I said, addressing my followers by the name I'd given them. "I'm here at *Trouble*. It's not a new spot but it's got a new owner and shit is definitely poppin' in here for all of you who may still be looking for something to get into tonight! The DJ is—"

Before I could finish my sentence, my eyes went to the right of my screen as a chocolatey pussy throbbing, hunk of a man came into view right behind me. Wrapping his arms around me, he sat his chin on my shoulder and looked into my screen.

"What's good?" he said before I ended the live stream and pulled away from his grasp to look at him. And damn, was he *fine*. Standing tall like an NBA basketball player, he lowered his beautiful brown eyes and stared at me blankly before wetting his lips with his tongue and pulling his thick, succulent lips into a smirk. Blinking fast, I fought to gain my composure.

"Um… excuse me but do I know you?" I snapped with attitude once I found my voice.

Yes, he had the looks to fulfill nearly every woman's fantasies but he'd placed his hands where they didn't belong and needed to be checked for the intrusion—no matter how comfortable his big, beefy arms had felt around my… Oh shit—I had to stop the madness or I was really going to get my ass beat.

"You don't, but I know you," was his simple reply as his eyes liberally scanned my body before finding my face. "I'm Trevor."

He held his hand out for mine but I wasn't about to yield to him that easily. Pushing his hand away, I crossed my arms in front of my body and placed my weight to one side. Out of the corner of my eye, I saw Bryan heading quickly in our direction, probably to remind me that I was here to do a job and needed to squash the bullshit so I could hurry up and get to it.

"No, what you are is disrespectful and you not gon' be putting your hands—"

"Carmella!" Bryan gasped, grabbing me by the shoulder just as I was about to get in Trevor's ass. My eyes went to him and he gave me a wide-eyed look before turning towards Trevor who was standing with his arms crossed in front of his chest and a sly smirk on his face, as if he had been enjoying the fire I was giving him.

"Carmella… this is *Trevor*," he informed me with a pointed eye and I stared blankly back at him, wondering what that was supposed to mean to me. "Trevor... the owner of this club. He's the one who contacted me about you coming here."

My lips parted slightly as my eyes went from Bryan's to Trevor. His smirk was gone but he didn't appear angry or put off. Raising his hand to his face, he ran it over his mouth and continued to look at me under his low, sleepy eyelids. Got*damn* his ass was all kinds of sexy.

"I see. Well, it's nice to meet you, Trevor. I just don't take kindly to being touched by men I don't know."

Unfolding my arms, I placed my hand out towards him and waited. He bent his eyes to look at it and then chuckled a little before grabbing it, pulling it up to his lips, and kissing it softly.

"Nice to meet you. And excuse the intrusion."

He ran his tongue over his lower row of teeth in a way that made me feel faint. I had to get the hell out of this club and quick. There was a reason this club was named 'Trouble' because that was exactly what I was going to get into if I didn't get myself together.

"It's nothing," I replied nonchalantly while pressing my lips together in a forced smile. "I have a job to do so I'm going to get to it."

Turning around, I walked away, trying my hardest to ignore the fact that I knew Trevor's eyes were on me every step of the way. Bryan appeared at my side the second I sat down at the bar, but I avoided his eyes. Since being with Cree, no man had ever been able to make me feel the way that I was feeling now. I didn't know what it was about Trevor, but he had my ass shook.

"Damn!" Bryan let out breathlessly from beside me. "That muthafucka right there shole is fine!"

Bunching my lips together, I turned to look at him but refused to reply right away. Thankfully, my phone vibrated in my hand, saving me from admitting that Trevor wasn't just fine—he was *fine as hell.*

Cree: Aye, what you up to?

Rolling my eyes, I sighed and shook my head before looking back down at the screen. This nigga wasn't slick. It wasn't a coincidence that only minutes after my live video ended, featuring Trevor who decided to make a quick cameo, Cree was hitting me up. He hadn't bothered to message me all night, but here he was.

I'm working, was my simple reply.

Cree: Work's over. Get home. Now.

Can you believe his nerve? Like for real! He could go where he wanted without telling me where he was or what he was doing, but the second I did something he didn't approve of, he wanted to shut me down. Not happening; I was my own woman today just like I'd been when I met him.

I'll be home when I'm done with what I need to do.

After that I turned my phone on 'Do Not Disturb' to stop him from blowing me up like I knew he would until he was sure that I was bringing my ass home. The problem with Cree is that he thought he could own me and that wasn't happening. Janelle and I were sisters but I wasn't her. Outlaw could tell her ass to do something and, just like the obedient soul she was, she'd do just as he asked. She might even cop an attitude but she'd still do what was asked of her and she'd always been that way ever since we were kids.

Me, on the other hand? I wasn't for that bullshit! A muthafucka could talk all day about what I better do and I'd still do whatever the hell I wanted in the end. Ask George Jefferson Pickney if you don't believe me. If my daddy couldn't tell me what to do, Cree definitely couldn't.

"Oh shit!! This is my song!"

I giggled as Bryan jumped up and started dancing hard as hell with jerky motions to the song the DJ was spinning. We'd been in the club for about thirty minutes and we were still sitting at the bar. Sitting around was something I never did this long while working but, for some reason, I wasn't comfortable getting on the dancefloor, thinking that I might run into Trevor again. However, I hadn't seen a trace of him for the last thirty minutes—and I had definitely been looking for him—so I shrugged and stood up with Bryan, thinking it was probably safe to get back to enjoying myself.

"I love this song too," I admitted and started dancing in the center of the floor. Some of the people around seemed to recognize me and backed away a little to give me some space. I ignored everyone around as a few people began to whisper to each other and take pictures or video while I danced. This was the life of being somewhat of a local celebrity. I took it all in stride.

The lights were dim and the beat was right, giving a natural high that felt even better than any drug had ever made me feel. Closing my eyes, I began to wind my body to the beat and shook my head from side-to-side, enjoying the feel of the bass thumping in my body. Before I knew it, I felt soft lips on my neck before an arm wrapped around my waist. A firm body pressed against the back of mine and swayed in sync with me, catching the rhythm of my hips.

I knew it was him without even looking. Even before the scent of his cologne entered my nostrils and created a river in my already damp panties.

Damn.

Relaxing into him, I continued dancing and his grip became firmer as he tugged backwards, pressing me closer against his body. I needed to pull away but I couldn't because I didn't want to. Wasn't nothing wrong with dancing, right?

"Carm!"

Even the sound of alarm in Bryan's voice couldn't wake me from the hypnotic state I was in. My mind had blocked everything out and the only thing I could focus on was his body on mine and mine on his as we danced to the beat. But damn, if he could dance like this, I wonder how it would be if we fu—

"Carmella!" Bryan said with more urgency before grabbing my arm and shaking it hard, successfully jerking me out of my trance.

"What?" I snapped, not meaning to but it came out that way anyways. Stepping forward, I pushed Trevor's arms from around my waist before glancing at him and cutting my eyes quickly away when I noted the desire in his.

"Bitch! Cree is coming this way!"

I scrunched up my nose and leaned closer, certain that I hadn't heard Bryan correctly. "Huh?"

"Cree, bitch! He's here!"

My eyes widened and my heart dropped to my toes as I turned around and followed Bryan's eyes. Sure enough, Cree was marching towards me, his brows bunched together across his forehead and a vicious scowl on his face. His eyes, however, weren't on me.

"Oh shit…" I whispered, barely moving my lips.

"Bitch ruuuuunnnn!" Bryan urged from beside me, pushing hard on my shoulder, but I didn't move. I was stuck in place, unable to turn away from the train wreck that I knew was coming. I heard the sound of platform shoes on tile floors, clacking away in the distance behind me and I turned, seeing Bryan running away with his arms in the air waving above his head. So much for being my ride or die.

"Da fuck you doin', nigga?!" Cree snapped as soon as he was standing in front of Trevor, holding up his shirt to show the pistol stashed at his side. "You need to watch ya fuckin' hands before I body yo' ass in this bitch."

Cree gritted on Trevor for a second before pushing him to the side like he wasn't shit and focusing his attention on me.

"And as for you," he started, pointing his index finger square in the center of my chest hard enough to make me stagger back a little. "Take yo' dumb ass home before—"

Before Cree could finish his sentence, I felt the atmosphere shift around me. The music was still thumping but no one around me was dancing. Once I pulled my eyes from his to look around, I saw that we were surrounded by three men who had come out of nowhere, dressed in all black, their faces pulled into tight frowns, arms heavily tattooed.

Without showing a shred of fear, Cree backed away from me

and looked at each one of them with a menacing stare that said he was ready to go if they were too. Chuckling a little to himself, Trevor stepped up and stood with his shoulders squared and his eyes on Cree.

"You think you gon' run shit in my fuckin' club, Cree?" Trevor asked and I squinted my eyes at him. He knew Cree?

"I don't give a fuck what yo' last name is… this right here is my shit!"

The same question I had seemed to be running through Cree's mind because he paused for a beat and his eyes pulled tight as he glared back at Trevor. I saw him bite down on his back teeth, obviously annoyed that he couldn't place his face.

"Y'all muthafuckas move out my fuckin' way 'fore I air this bitch out!"

My head turned towards a voice that I knew all too well. Nudging a woman out of the way by pushing the back of her head hard enough to set her feet in motion, Outlaw stepped up with his gun in hand, screw-face in place, and his signature threatening glare in his eyes.

"Outlaw, huh? I should've known you wouldn't have come here on your own, Cree." Trevor snorted, his smirk still in place as he shook his head. "You always gotta have lil' bruh around to protect you, huh?"

"Who da fuck is *this* off-brand ass nigga, Cree?" Outlaw frowned as he wandered a few more steps forward, using the barrel of his gun to point at Trevor. Trevor's men lifted their weapons in response, aiming them directly at Outlaw, and I felt my knees tremble.

"Back down. Put your weapons up," Trevor commanded them, lifting his hand. "Outlaw ain't gon' do shit in front of all these witnesses."

"Call my bluff then, nigga," was all Outlaw said and even I had to wonder how crazy his ass really was. Apparently, Trevor was wondering the same thing because he moved his attention from Outlaw to Cree and decided to answer Outlaw's question.

"They call me Vick," he said and I watched the light flicker in Cree's eyes. "You know the name, don't you?"

"Shit don't ring no bells with me," Outlaw replied nonchalantly before opening up his clip and counting his bullets.

Ignoring Outlaw, Trevor continued to focus on Cree. "You thought you could just fuck my bitch and I wouldn't do shit 'cause I was locked up, huh? Well, I'm out now so what yo' punk ass gon' do 'bout—"

Crack!

Before I could even process what was happening, Outlaw raised his gun and swung it all the way from California to the Florida coast, smashing it hard against the side of Trevor's head. With a gash steadily oozing blood, Trevor dropped to the ground at the same moment that his men went to grab their pieces. I screamed and dove for cover before turning around to look for Bryan who was nowhere to be found.

Click! Click! Click!

Seemingly out of nowhere, Yolo, Tank, and Kane each appeared to their sides and pressed the barrel of their cocked guns to each of the three men's temples.

"Live to fight another day. This ain't for y'all and you and yo' family don't want these problems," Kane told the men before motioning to Outlaw. "And Luke, you ain't have to do that shit! Let's get da hell outta here."

Before moving, Outlaw kicked at Trevor's legs, his lips curled up in disgust. "Maybe I didn't, but the nigga was talkin' too greasy for me."

When Cree's eyes landed on mine, he didn't give me a chance to make a move or say a single word before snatching me up by the arm and nearly dragging me out of the club. Swallowing hard, I struggled to keep up with his pace, asking myself why the hell I'd put myself in this position. I should've known that things wouldn't work out in my favor because I knew the type of nigga I was dealing with. Just like Bryan said… Cree definitely didn't have it all when it came to my pretty ass.

Pretty *dumb* ass.

Sidney

God, I hate this.

Feeling like a toddler walking on stilts, I reeled forward through the crowded club, praying to God every step of the way that I didn't fall forward and bust my face. Who knew that being a woman meant I'd be sentenced to a life of discomfort, all for the sake of pleasing a man? I definitely didn't and it was something I'd fought against every second of my existence until I became Yolo's girl. Now, instead of rocking Js on my feet, a fitted cap, True Religion jeans, and a simple tee, I was wearing heels, dresses, tights, and whatever tight ass outfit he bought for me to squeeze in.

"Relax your face, sis. You look like you're taking a shit." Doubling over, Teema laughed hard at my expense, not even offering a hand amidst my struggle. Now ain't that some shit?

"Hush and let me get your arm before you have to scrape my ass up off the floor," I told her before latching on to her side without permission. "Yolo's ass ain't even here. I could've worn what the hell I wanted to from the beginning."

Rolling her beautiful browns to the ceiling before landing them on my face, Teema pursed her lips in disapproval before speaking.

"A man like Yolo doesn't want his woman walking around here in his clothes. And it wouldn't hurt you to actually *look* like a woman sometimes."

"A man like Yolo who says he loves a woman like me shouldn't want me to change just to be with him!" I retorted, repeating the same sad ass line I used whenever I complained to Teema and she took his side. "Why can't I just be me?"

She pressed her lips together once more but didn't respond, probably because she was saving her strength to continue half-carrying me across the room. Once we got to the section reserved for the Murrays, I sat down quickly, kicked off my heels and began massaging the soles of my feet with my hands.

"You're like the person who cries about being poor then wins the lotto and starts to cry about how hard it is to manage all that money." When I gave Teema a blank stare, she explained further. "You asked for something and now you want to complain about the conditions that are required to keep it. Nobody made you decide to be with Yolo!"

Pouting in silence, I turned away and looked over the crowd before stuffing my feet into my heels and slumping down in my seat. She was right, but I didn't want to hear it. I wanted everything my way but, when it came to relationships—especially relationships with the Murray crew—you couldn't have everything your way.

"I'm just saying… I don't like dressing like this all the time. I like the person I used to be."

Something about what I said must have finally hit Teema in a way that made her understand because she sighed and turned around to face me, the expression on her face a lot softer than before.

"I know how you feel," she told me before pausing a bit as if contemplating if she wanted to tell me something. "Before getting with Kane, I didn't depend on a man for shit. In fact, he was the reason for that because of how things ended between us. After leaving him, I vowed that I would only depend on me and me alone to provide for myself and my daughter. Now I'm married and, even though I'm happy about that, I have no career… I feel like I'm not doing anything with my life. I prided myself on being independent but now I don't feel like I'm that anymore."

"But you aren't dependent on Kane. Yes, he works and brings in the money but you're still your own person. Being a stay-at-home mom doesn't change who you are."

"And clothes don't change who you are," she told me with a pointed expression. "Women do a lot of shit we don't like to do in order to keep a man. Shit, we wouldn't do if it didn't matter to them or help us keep these thirsty bitches from being able to get up in their face. But at the end of the day, when you take all that shit off, he is still in love with you. Any bitch out here can put on a dress and shake her ass in front of Yolo but he likes it when you do it. Don't get it twisted. If that nigga didn't love your ass for you, you could put on a dress and heels all day and he still wouldn't give a shit."

As soon as she said that, my eyes went to the doors of the club as they opened wide and I felt my heart flutter when in walked Yolo, followed closely behind by Kane and Outlaw. I watched as all eyes turned to watch them as they pushed through the crowd, stopping every now and then to dap somebody up or speak. Then, under my watchful eye, a chick wearing a form-fitting yellow dress with curves for days walked up and grabbed Yolo on his arm, tugging him slightly so that he looked at her.

My chest burned as I watched them speak, but I tried to keep my cool, knowing that eyes were on me and appearing jealous would mean that I had something to worry about when it came to my man. Definitely not what I needed to portray in front of these hoes. The girl leaned close to Yolo, whispering in his ear to ensure that she was heard over the loud music in the club, and Yolo nodded his head at whatever she was saying. The most sensitive of the Murrays, Yolo was never one to be rude so I wasn't the least bit surprised that he was giving this girl the time of day but still, I didn't like it.

Once they'd finished their brief conversation that seemed to carry on for far too long, in my opinion, Yolo's eyes landed on my face and he made a bee-line to me. I hated the way that looking at him changed my entire mood. No matter how much I tried to be mad at him or pissed off by something he did, he managed to change everything with one look.

Stepping up to me, he leaned down and kissed me passionately on the lips, long and sweet as if there was no one else around. When he pulled away, my eyes fluttered as I fought to catch my breath.

"You're fuckin' gorgeous." He eyed me up and down, licking his lips hungrily, and I instantly forgot all about how much I hated dresses and heels. I'd sleep in them bitches if it kept this same look in his eyes. Glancing over to where Teema was posted up with Kane, I saw a smirk on her face and I nodded my head slightly, letting her know that everything she'd told me was right on point.

Yolo sat at my side and grabbed my hand, kissing the top of it softly before placing it in his lap. He was forever the romantic and I couldn't help but love it. Still, I was curious about the woman I'd seen him with.

"Finish your conversation?"

Sipping from his cup, Yolo glanced in my direction with his brows bunched tight on his head.

"Hmm?"

I pointed my eyes over to where he'd been standing and then looked back at him.

"Oh…" Chuckling a little, he cocked his head to the side. "You jealous?"

A stinging sensation erupted in my chest and I grabbed his cup from his hand to take a sip and appear at ease. Still, I could feel his eyes on me and I knew I wasn't fooling anyone. Yolo knew me too well for me to hide anything from him. We'd been doing this love thing for too long.

"Don't pay these bitches no mind. No one out here got what you got."

I lifted a brow and pursed my lips. "What I got?"

He patted his chest firmly and spoke with sincerity. "My heart."

My love for him exploded inside of me, filling my entire body with warmth. Yolo wrapped his arms around me and pulled me into him, bringing me into the place where I felt peace. This was what it was supposed to feel like to be in love with someone. This was what I'd longed for since the day that I'd first laid eyes on Yolo, and now I finally had it.

"I know I ain't do right by you before, but that was just the stupid ass mistakes that a dumb ass kid makes. I'm a grown man, Sid. If I say we good, then we good."

Years of knowing Yolo and it still felt crazy to me that he could pick up on my thoughts, my mood, and my fears without me saying a word.

"Believe me?" he asked, pulling away so that he could look me in my eyes.

"I believe you."

***

"Come on, Mama, it's time for you to eat."

"I done told you once and I done told yo' baldheaded ass twice... I ain't eatin' that shit!"

"Mama, I'm not baldheaded!" I argued, pulling at my long ponytail. She glared at me so menacingly that I thought I saw a preview of the afterlife.

"You will be if you keep messin' with me, girl!"

Sighing, I placed my hands on my hips and shook my head at Grandma Murray. Her eyes were rested on my face, with the same stubborn glare in them that had been inherited by each of her grandsons.

"You have to eat. Please, don't make this difficult for me," I pleaded with my hands together as if in prayer.

"Chile, you makin' this difficult for yourself. I done told you I ain't eatin' that tasteless shit so you might as well get the hell on."

With that, she poked her lips out and crossed her arms in front of her chest, lifting her chin up high in the air. I sighed deeply and plopped down in the chair across the table from her. She wasn't going to budge.

After learning from Yolo that Grandma Murray had been diagnosed with high blood pressure, it only took a few visits to her house for dinner to see why. Grandma Murray cooked just like any grandmother in the hood, her food was good on taste but heavy on the salt. After speaking to her about her health, I realized that even though she knew that the food she ate was hurting her health, she had no intentions of changing so I started taking it upon myself to come over each day to make sure that she was eating well.

"Okay, fine. I'll let you put a little seasoning on it. But just a bit." My attempt at a compromise. "You have to understand, I'm doing this to help you. We don't want nothing happening to you, Mama."

Her facial expression relaxed a little but she kept her arms folded and her chin high in the air, still avoiding my eyes. I shook my head and grabbed the salt and pepper, dumping a little in my hand before sprinkling it over her grits and eggs and then mixing it in. I caught her eyes drop slightly to observe me as I seasoned her food.

"Good?"

"Humph!" she huffed, but by the time I sat back down in my chair, she was picking up her fork to give it a taste.

Before placing the forkful of food into her mouth, she bent her head down and sniffed it a couple times as if she could tell whether it was seasoned right by the smell. Rolling my eyes, I bit my lip to stop the smile from coming up on my face. I just couldn't with this woman. I loved her to death but she was crazy as hell.

"Girl, what side of you got white in you?" she asked and I curled my brows in confusion.

"Huh?"

"I said," she began, pointing the fork at me, "what side of you got white folks? Because us black folks don't put seasoning in our hands and sprinkle it on food."

"I'm just trying to make sure you stay healthy, Mama. The doctor said—"

"The doctor don't know shit! My daddy ate what he wanted until the day he died. Every morning my mama would cook a pile of bacon for him and he'd eat it all by himself. Now, white folks will tell you that bacon will kill you, give you cholesterol, the sugars, and all that fancy shit. But my daddy lived until he was—"

I smiled and listened to Grandma Murray as she rattled on about how her family ate and how long they lived as if it was the first time I was hearing it. She told me the same thing every day, and I listened just as I was now, because as long as she was eating the food I'd made for her, I didn't mind hearing her complain about it. By the time she finished her story, all of the food I gave her would be gone.

"Now what's goin' on with you and my grandson? You keepin' him happy?"

I smiled. "Yes, ma'am."

"Good," was all she said.

Shaking my head at her, I sighed and grabbed my phone. She never asked me if Yolo was keeping me happy because she didn't even care if he was. Just like her offspring, Grandma Murray's primary concern was for her family and whether or not her boys were being taken care of. If you did right by them, you were good in her book. If not, she didn't give a damn about you.

"Okay, well, I'll be back tomorrow. I have to get to work and I'll probably be there late today. I left your lunch and dinner in the refrigerator."

She curled up her nose in disgust at my mention of food, but I ignored it. The salt was tucked in my backpack and I knew she wasn't going to go out to buy any more so, regardless to the look on her face, she would be eating what I prepared for her exactly how I'd prepared it. Leaning over, I kissed her on the cheek and she gave me an affectionate pat on the butt when I turned to leave.

"I would tell you to put on somethin' to cover your tail but it's nice to see you in somethin' other than them long ass shorts for once. Who knew you had all that booty? Well… I guess Young Yellow did."

She wiggled her brows suggestively at me and I giggled at her before walking out the door. As soon as I stuck my key into the door of my car, I had a feeling that someone was looking at me. Lifting my head, my eyes connected with the driver of a car that was passing by and I froze in place, immediately recognizing the face. It was the chick from the club, the one who had been speaking to Yolo, but I didn't remember where I knew her from until the car had made a right around the corner.

Frowning deeply, I sat down in my car and then turned the key in the ignition, feeling like something wasn't right. But then I shook my head and pushed my worries away. The club we were at was in Brooklyn, only a couple blocks from Yolo's grandma's house so maybe the girl just lived in the neighborhood. Maybe I was worrying myself about nothing at all.

Janelle

*T*here was a knock at my office door that interrupted my thoughts and when I looked up, I saw that it was Gerald.

"Come in," I said with a wave of my hand.

I knew from the look on his face that Gerald was coming to give me bad news. Every day it was bad news and the more that I had to deal with it, the harder it became to even walk into my office each day.

"I'm sorry to say this, Janelle, but…"

"Just say it."

Gerald sighed and sat down in the chair in front of my desk. "We lost another account. A pretty big one."

"Did they say why?" My voice came out more like a whine than I'd wanted it to.

"Um…" His eyes averted mine and he shifted in his seat, his brown skin looking a little paler than normal. I could read him easily. He didn't want to tell me it was because of Luke… my relationship had cost me again.

Lowering my head, I placed my face in my hands and let out a breath before pulling back up, reminding myself that I couldn't break down. I had a business to run.

"I'm going to go to spend this week meeting up with the clients that we have left… making sure they are satisfied so we can stay afloat." Gerald gave me a weak smile and I wondered how far his loyalty would go before it was spread too thin. We had become friends during the time we'd worked together, but friendship didn't pay the bills and Gerald was good at what he did. He could easily get a job at another firm and make triple what he was making now.

"That's a good idea," I told him. "And thanks for doing it."

Reaching over the top of my desk, Gerald placed his hand over mine and his weak smile grew larger on his face, nearly spreading up to his kind eyes. I smiled as well, feeling somewhat relieved under the intense pressure. Although Luke seemed to think there was something to worry about when it came to Gerald, it couldn't be more untrue. Gerald was a friend and nothing more. He understood what I was going through and helped me through it, but I never got the feeling that he was trying to be my man or threaten my relationship. He just wanted to help.

Leaning back in my chair, I watched as Gerald stood up to walk out of my office. Once he closed the door behind him, I realized that I was being watched as well. My eyes tugged towards the right and landed right on Sidney who was looking at me through the glass wall between us. Without knocking, she walked in and plopped right down in the chair that Gerald had just vacated.

"I think you should tell Outlaw."

I frowned. "Tell him what?"

With her head cocked to the side, she rolled her eyes like she was annoyed. "Tell him about what is going on here with your business.

You're keeping it from him but you know he can help."

Crinkling my nose, I shook my head. "I don't need him bailing me out. I've got this, Sid."

Her eyes widened. "Oh, you've got this? You forget that part of my job is to go over your finances. You *don't* have this, Janelle."

"And you want me to tell Luke that the reason I'm losing clients is because of him? We lost five corporate accounts because they found out that—"

"Maybe that's your problem, Janelle," she started, leaning back in her chair and crossing her arms in front of her chest. "If your clients have a problem with you because of who your nigga is, fuck 'em. You need to focus on landing clients who don't give a shit. Make that Murray name work for you. There are a lot of muthafuckas who would want you because you represent the Murrays. Stop focusing on the people who don't."

My eyes pulled tight. "But how do I find people like that?"

Pursing her lips, she cocked her head to the side and widened her eyes, speaking with no words.

"I have to talk to Luke, huh?"

"You're getting married to him… y'all are a team. You need to use that shit to your advantage!"

Letting out a forced laugh, I had to admit that she was right. I wasn't the type to ask for help from anyone, but maybe it was time for that to change. Sidney stood up to leave and I was about to let her go when a thought crossed my mind.

"Sidney, wait!" She stopped and looked at me, waiting. Folding my lips into my mouth, I wondered if I should tell her what I was thinking. And then I sighed and decided to go ahead and do it. I couldn't keep things in any longer. It was driving me crazy.

"I got an email a couple weeks ago from some bitch Luke used to mess with. She sent a video… a sex tape of the two of them messing around."

"What?!" Sidney dropped back down in her seat and looked at me with her mouth wide open. "You *sure* it's him?"

I nodded my head. "I only watched about five seconds of it, but I heard his voice. I know it's him. It's from before we were officially together so I didn't say anything to him about it."

"Well, who is the girl?" she asked and I paused for a minute, crinkling my brows together. After cutting the video off, I never thought to go back to see if the woman's face eventually popped up in the video. Once I saw it was Luke, I had no desire to go back and look at the rest.

"I—I don't know. The part I saw… her face wasn't showing. She was ass up and—" A stinging feeling went through my chest as I thought back to it. "—he was behind her. I turned it off as soon as I saw it was him. I couldn't bring myself to watch the rest."

"Well, let me see it," Sidney replied nonchalantly as if she weren't asking for me to hand over a tape of my man long-stroking some other bitch.

"What?!" I gawked at her. "I'm not letting you see no video of Luke fuckin' some other girl!"

"Janelle, you don't want to look at it but you need to know who this bitch is that's sending you videos. Even if it's from before y'all were together, for some reason, she's trying to get at you and she needs to get her ass beat. Ignoring it won't make it go away."

I couldn't argue with that.

With my lips pressed firmly together, I grabbed my computer and went to my email. After scrolling for a while just to stall for time, I went to the folder where I'd stashed the video and hovered the mouse over it.

"Go ahead and click it," Sidney pressed from where she'd taken a seat by my side. I closed my eyes, took a breath and clicked on the email before double-clicking to play the video.

It began to play and I felt my insides knot up when I began to hear Luke's moans of pleasure. Tears came to my eyes as I watched him please another woman in the way that he pleased me. I couldn't even look at anything on the screen but him. Even if he hadn't been with me at the time, it still seemed like a betrayal that he'd given himself to someone other than me.

"Ohhhh Luke!" the woman on the video called out, and I frowned and squinted at the screen once I'd heard her voice for the first time. Although the sound wasn't all that good and her voice was a little muffled, something about it seemed so familiar.

"Throw it back on me," Luke demanded through clenched teeth as he fucked her from behind. "Do that shit... daaaaamn."

I squeezed my eyes closed as the girl in the video moaned hard, utterly enjoying every bit of what he was shoving up inside of her. I couldn't look at it anymore. I refused.

"Um... Janelle?" Sidney's voice wavered a little when she said my name and I had the feeling that something was wrong.

"Huh?"

Wiping away a tear, I opened my eyes but still couldn't bring my eyes to the screen so I looked in Sidney's face instead. Like me, she was no longer looking at the screen either and, instead had her wide eyes pinned on mine as the video continued to play.

"Um… I think—I think you need to watch this alone."

"Huh?" I repeated.

"Fuck… Janelle, this pussy so fuckin' good!" Luke growled out and I shot my eyes to my laptop.

Luke had switched positions and instead of hitting it up from the back, he was hovering over the top of the screen with a thigh over his shoulder as he thrust his hips back and forth. The woman who had seemed so familiar to me was now laying on her back, titties in the air—titties that I instantly recognized because they were mine.

"Oh my god…"

As soon as I realized what I was watching the camera shifted and the focus was on my face. I was deep in the thralls of absolute pleasure, in full fuck-face mode, eyes pulled tight, mouth wide open, enjoying every second of what Luke was giving to me. A few seconds later, the video cut off and everything went black before words appeared.

You screwed me over by screwing him, and now I'm going to make sure you're screwed too.

The video went to a screen recording of someone creating an email. The video of me and Luke was added as an attachment before a series of email addresses were added. I immediately recognized the email addresses as belonging to some of my former top clients.

"Shit!" Sidney said as she watched from beside me, realizing at the same time that I did what was happening.

A short message was entered into the body of the email, *"Look what your amazing attorney has been up to,"* before the message was sent. I was frozen into place, not believing what I was seeing, not understanding why someone would do this to me. But here it was and I was finally understanding a few things. I'd lost my clients not because of Luke's reputation or anything he'd done. I'd lost my clients because of me.

"This video was never about Luke," I said when I was finally able to find my voice. "It was about me."

"Do you know who sent it?" Sidney's voice was a hushed whisper, like she was keeping a secret. But there was no need for her to whisper now. I thought back to Gerald and how uncomfortable he'd seemed when I asked why our clients were leaving. I'd assumed it was about Luke, but that wasn't it. He knew about the video. And there was no telling who else knew about it too.

"Yeah, I know who sent it," I replied, leaning back in my chair. I pressed my fingers over the top of my forehead, an attempt to relieve some pressure. Shit didn't work.

"It's Val. My old roommate." I bit down on the side of my lip and shook my head. "When I got with Luke, she took it personally... almost stood by and let some niggas rape me in our living room. Luke found out about it and kicked her out." I left out the fact that Luke and his brothers had most likely killed the man involved who had been dating Val at the time. "I should've known that she wouldn't let things go so easily, but I wasn't expecting this. Why would she want to ruin my life?"

Shaking her head, Sidney looked at my computer screen with a grim expression on her face. "I don't know, but I think you need to find that bitch and ask her."

Luke

I took a deep breath before walking in the house, wondering if Janelle was going to be on some crazy shit that would have me ready to strangle her ass. But when I was greeted by the scent of some good ass food and Jill Scott songs playing over the intercoms inside, the corner of my lips pulled up into a half-smile. She was in a good mood. A nigga might get lucky tonight.

"You hungry?"

I turned around from taking off my shoes and saw Janelle standing behind me in some sexy lingerie and my man below rocked up instantly. It didn't matter to me that she was pregnant with a belly so big she couldn't see her toes. Every part of her looked sexy to me and what I felt for her was even more intense than it had been before. She was carrying my baby inside of her and soon, she would even be my wife. This was the type of shit a thug prayed for.

"Yeah, I'm hungry," I replied, looking below her waist. She giggled and ducked her head a little to catch my eyes.

"I mean for food, Luke. I cooked for you." Her eyes sparkled as she spoke and I couldn't help but think about how much I missed her like this. If she stayed on this sweet shit, she could get anything she wanted from a nigga, I swear. This was what I liked to come home to. Fuck fighting every damn day. Even if the make-up sex was on fire, I'd give it up without a second thought to forever have days like this.

"I don't mind having dinner before dessert."

Her face lit up. "Turn off your phone. I don't want any interruptions."

I lifted her chin with my finger and crushed her lips to mine, licking and sucking before I pulled away. Her cherry lipgloss had me wanting to double back for more, but I controlled myself, knowing that Janelle had probably planned the order of the evening and her organized ass hated for things not to go how she had planned them.

I was on my second plate when the doorbell rang. Janelle's ass didn't cook often but when she did, the shit was bomb. She told me that after her mama died, it was her responsibility to help her daddy out by cooking dinner most nights. Since we'd started living together, she didn't cook often because she worked so much but every now and then, she'd show a nigga her skills.

"I'll answer it," she said, jumping up from her chair and I gave her a look that said everything I was thinking before I even opened my mouth. Rolling her eyes, she sat back down in her chair and continued eating.

"Yo' ass know that you don't answer no damn doors when I'm home. I got this shit…" Standing up, I wiped my mouth with a napkin but kept my eyes on her. She let out a heavy breath and then smirked, but didn't say shit.

"You expectin' a nigga to come over here or somethin'? You jumped up fast as hell. Shakin' up my damn baby girl."

"Just answer the damn door, Luke!"

Chuckling, I walked to the front door wondering which one of my brothers was stopping by without calling first. Cree and Yolo did that shit all the damn time so it was probably one of them. Or maybe Kane had got home after curfew and Teema tossed his ass out.

"Shit!" I said once I looked out the blinds and saw who it was standing at the front door. Running my hand over my face, I unlocked it quickly and snatched it open.

"Pops, what's up? What you doin' here?"

Pops wasn't my pops, he was actually my home boy's father who owned a wing spot, named Pops, that I went to pretty often. After his son, J-Burg, got locked up, I gave Pops the money he needed to open the wing spot so that he could take care of himself and his daughter, Briyana. One thing I always liked about Pops was that no matter what he was going through, he always had a smile on his face.

But not this time. Pop's looked like he'd been stressing for a minute, his complexion looking paler than normal, almost lifeless. The corners of his eyes tugged down in sadness and his facial hair was unkempt and overgrown like he hadn't been taking care of himself for a while.

"I—I begged Tank to tell me where you stayed. We tried callin' but got no answer. He brought me over here."

It was then that I looked at the car behind him and saw that it was my brother's. Lifting my hand, I gave Tank a signal that it was fine for him to leave before turning my attention back to Pops. I backed away from the door to give him room to come in.

"Come on in, Pops."

Without a word, he stepped inside and I couldn't help noticing the way that he was wringing his hands together in worry. Something was up and I prayed to God that my nigga, J-Burg, hadn't got caught slipping in prison. We had ran the streets together and he was close to me, just like another brother. When he went in, I promised him that no matter what, I'd always take care of his family so he didn't have to worry.

I ushered Pops to the living room and waited for him to sit down before I sat down across from him.

"Tell me what's goin' on."

Before speaking, he pushed his lips firmly together, pulled his glasses from his face and rubbed at his eyes wearily before replacing the thick glasses over the top of his wide nose.

"It's Bri-Bri," he started, referring to his daughter. "She... she started messin' with some drug dealer out in Harlem. I've been tryin' to let her make her own mistakes and not interfere, but she's been callin' me less and less. Now I can't get in contact with her at all. I—I asked around and..." He paused and took his glasses off once more to rub at his red eyes. "I hear that he got her out there sellin' her body for him. I don't know what to do... I—I know if her brother were around, she wouldn't be doin' this. I'm tryin' to do right by her but..."

He lost it and collapsed into a fit of tears. I heard motion behind me and then Janelle appeared by my side with a box of tissues. I nodded, letting her know that she wasn't overstepping, and she walked over to Pops, rubbing his back as she handed him a few tissues so that he could clean his face.

"She's all I have left. Jimmy's gonna be gone for the rest of his life and… I promised their mother that I would take care of our children. I've failed!"

Leaning forward, I waited for Pops to get himself together a little before continuing our conversation. Janelle sat on the arm of his chair and continued rubbing his back.

"Would you like a glass of water?" she asked and Pops nodded his head. I waited for her to walk away before I spoke.

"Who has her?"

"That drug dealer everyone talks about out there… I think his name is Remy."

I knew the nigga, Remy. Didn't have no issues with him because we didn't operate in the same circles. He ran the streets selling drugs and I took shit. Our paths never really crossed. Still, I knew that if he had Briyana out on the hoe stroll, he wasn't going to give her up easily. Remy wasn't my enemy and we didn't have beef, but we would soon.

Janelle walked back into the room, holding a glass of ice water in her hand and handed it over to Pops who drank it quickly, as if he hadn't had anything to drink in a while.

"Let me take you home, Pops. I don't want you worryin' about this shit anymore either, okay? It'll be fine."

Pops nodded his head in relief, but Janelle cut her eyes at me, giving me a pointed expression that I couldn't quite read, but I knew meant that she wasn't in agreement about something.

"Would you like something to eat before you go?" Janelle asked and Pops looked at me before nodding his head. "Come on, I'll show you to the dining room."

After fixing Pops a plate, Janelle came back into the room and sat down, saying nothing as I texted back and forth on the phone. I knew some niggas in Harlem who could tell me exactly where to find Remy and let me know what was going on with Briyana.

"You gon' tell me what's on your mind or you gon' just sit there and stare at a nigga?" I placed my phone down and looked at Janelle, knowing from the look on her face that she had a lot to say.

"I hope you aren't going to Harlem to confront no drug dealer, Luke." She folded her arms in front of her chest and waited for me to respond, but I didn't say anything, only looked back at her.

"I'm serious, Luke!"

Sighing, I sat back in my chair and thought out my words carefully before responding. There was a lot that Janelle still didn't know about me, things that she would have to learn with time. In the past, I'd done a lot of reckless shit—it was why Kane stayed on my ass. People in the hood were a witness to a lot of the things we all did. We'd earned our reputation through terror, running the streets, doing what we wanted, and canceling any niggas who got in our way.

But the reason that my brothers and I were able to do the shit that we did without ever getting caught was because the hood never gave us up. And the reason they never gave us up was because we took care of them. We operated in the space where the law failed and created our own standard of justice.

"What you don't understand is that I have a responsibility to people other than you," I told Janelle with an even tone. "As a lawyer, your responsibility is to the law. When people get in trouble with the law, muthafuckas call on you to get them out of it. As a street nigga, my responsibility lies with my hood. When bad shit happens in my hood, people call on me and my brothers to handle it for them… to set shit straight."

Shaking her head, Janelle looked at me with pleading eyes. "But this isn't your battle. This is why we have police and—"

I laughed, cutting her off. "Police? You expect Pops to call the police on a nigga like Remy? What you think gon' happen then?"

Cutting her eyes away briefly, she licked her lips and spoke carefully through her thoughts. "Well, they will go investigate and if they find out that what Pops says is true, they'll prosecute Remy and—"

"No, that's where you're wrong. Everything isn't so black and white, Nell. There are gray areas and you need to recognize it when you see it. Remy won't get locked up for shit, but what you think gon' happen to Pops once Remy finds out that he put them boys on him?" I paused, knowing that even Janelle's green ass could understand what I was trying to say. "You gotta get your head out the clouds, ma. It ain't healthy to be that naïve."

My phone vibrated against the top of the end table near me and I grabbed it, quickly reading the screen. It was a location for where I could find Remy. Knowing it would take me a while to get all the way over to Harlem, I stood up and glanced at my watch.

"Take care of Pops until I get back. Just let him shower and use one of the free rooms after he's done."

The next person on my list to speak with was Tank. Even though I felt like I could handle a nigga like Remy on my own, Kane had a rule that we were never to go alone if we expected a confrontation. It was something he came up with after Tone was killed.

"Aye, bruh, you still close by? I need you to pull up on somethin' with me," I told him as I walked up the stairs to get suited up for what I was about to get into. I'd expected Janelle would be what I'd be getting into 'round this time, but my folks needed me so plans had to change.

Janelle

I'd just gotten the man Luke referred to as Pops asleep when I got a text from Sidney asking me if I knew what was going on and where the guys were headed. Even though I was a novice to a lot of things and also naïve, as Luke had so nicely put it, when it came to the street life, I knew enough to know that if Yolo hadn't told her where he was going, it wasn't my place to fill her in.

I don't know, I started to write, and then I thought about how I'd confided in her about the video and she'd not only been there for me but was also keeping it secret for me until I figured out what I was going to do.

Some man named Pops came over here and asked Luke to help him get his daughter.

I sent the message and then walked into the bathroom to brush my teeth. When I got back, I checked my messages and saw that Sidney had already replied.

Sid: Briyana?

Yeah…

Sid: Oh, I can't stand her nasty ass. Bitch been a hoe all her damn life.

Well, now I knew why Yolo hadn't told her what he was doing.

Placing the phone down, I grabbed my computer and opened it, pausing as I thought to myself about how I was going to find Val. She no longer worked at the pharmacy, something I'd discovered after swinging by there after work, and no one working there had any information on where to find her. I called the last number I had for her, but it now belonged to someone else. Pulling up Facebook, I searched her name but came up with nothing. Same thing happened when I went to Instagram. Everything led me to a dead end.

Since I was already on Instagram, I looked up Carmella's page to see what she'd been up to. Needless to say, her life was far more adventurous than mine. Every picture was of her partying at some new place and looking as beautiful as ever. While I was looking at her pictures, I noticed that she'd responded to someone's comment only a couple minutes before so I grabbed my phone and called her.

"Bitch, what are you doing awake? Isn't it past your bedtime?"

I rolled my eyes to the sky. "Is that any way to greet your older sister?"

"You're lucky I answered the phone. How you know I'm not over here being nasty with Cree?"

"Because I saw you on Instagram and I know that Cree probably is wherever Luke is right now."

She got quiet for a few seconds and then sighed. "Yeah, you're right. And even if he wasn't with his brothers, we wouldn't be doing nothing nasty anyways."

"Wanna talk about it?" I asked, getting comfortable in the bed.

"Ain't shit to say but that Cree's ass is crazy as hell. I was in the club the other day, working and—"

Carmella commenced to telling me the craziest story about how Cree had popped up on her, along with the rest of the Murray crew, and drug her out of the club. I flinched when she detailed a part about Luke knocking the shit out of some guy she'd been dancing with when they walked in, biting down on my lip to stop myself from voicing my concern. Luke sincerely felt that he was above the law.

"You can't do things like that, Carm. You know how Cree is and baiting him could end up getting him in trouble."

She sucked the skin off of her teeth. "You're always worried about somebody getting in trouble! What about the embarrassment I suffered? What about my job? I get paid to show up at the hottest spots and talk about them. Who is going to want me to come to their club if they gotta worry about my nigga showing up with his brothers, pulling out guns and shit?"

The whole thing sounded so insane to me that all I could do was laugh about it. "Carm, stop trying that man then. If he tells you to bring your ass home, bring your ass home!"

I stayed on the phone with Carmella talking about anything that came to mind, other than my sex tape. The embarrassment of that situation made me want to keep it as quiet as I possibly could. I heard a door slam shut outside of my window and I jumped up to look outside, happy to see that Luke was back home.

"Carm, let me call you later. Luke is back."

"Good, that means Cree should be coming in the door at any minute. Love you, sis."

"I love you too," I replied and hung up the call.

Watching from the window, I saw Luke peel off his bloody shirt, step out of his pants and shoes, dump everything in a black garbage bag, and toss it in his trunk. He grabbed another bag out of the trunk, opened it, and pulled out a fresh pair of clothes and shoes. Once he had everything on, he opened the back door of his car and scooped a woman up in his arms. She was thin, seemingly unconscious, and wrapped in a blanket.

The front door opened and I walked out of the room to look down at the living room from the stairs. Luke stomped in and laid the woman on top of our sofa. She curled her arms around her body and turned to look at him. I could see the adoration in her eyes from where I stood.

"Rest," he told her and she nodded her head.

"A—are you going to leave me?"

She seemed afraid about him leaving her behind. Instead of answering, he walked up and rubbed her lightly on the side of her face. It seemed to calm her a little and she closed her eyes, falling asleep only seconds later.

I felt like I was seeing something that I shouldn't have been. It was a strange feeling, watching my man tend to another woman and, even though I didn't feel like there was anything between them, I couldn't help but feel some kind of way about him feeling responsible for protecting someone other than me. With my gut twisted up, I turned around and walked back to my bedroom, got under the covers, and pretended to be asleep. Only a few minutes later, Luke walked in and I heard his steps pause at the foot of the bed. He was watching me, trying to figure out if I was awake.

"Stop all that damn actin', Nell. I know you're up."

"Did you kill anyone?" I asked without hesitation. I flipped around in the bed and pushed away the sheets, sitting up so that I could look Luke straight in his eyes. A sliver of moonlight peeked through our curtains and partially illuminated his face, giving him a ghastly look in the dark.

"I saw the bloody clothes that you took off before walking in here," I pressed on when he didn't respond to me. "Did you kill anyone in order to save her?"

"I didn't do anything I didn't have to do. And that's all I'll say."

That answer wasn't good enough for me, but I knew it was all that I would get. Once again, I was conflicted. I'd been raised by an attorney who believed in the law, justice, and rules. With age, my daddy's morals and principles became my own. At my core, I believed that adhering to the laws was how we kept order and not adhering to them brought about chaos and devastation. But here I was about to marry a man who believed that the laws were meant to be broken whenever he deemed it necessary.

"I don't think you get what it means to be an attorney. I don't think you respect what I do. You want me to understand you but you don't understand me at all. It's not okay for you to murder and hurt people, Luke! What about the families of the people you've killed? Do you not owe them anything?"

Luke's eyes flashed red as his anger flared, but I stood my ground, not flinching and not backing down.

"Don't talk to me about families, Nell. The system you believe in has killed far more muthafuckas than I ever could. I guess if I had a badge, you'd be cool with this shit, huh? You got cops killin' niggas just for breathing, judges handing out life sentences just to pad their bank accounts—" He paused and I could see that he was getting increasingly agitated. "Pelmington… you remember him? The muthafucka whose name you had all scribbled down in your notebooks like he was some judiciary god? He's on my muthafuckin' team now! He's doin' what the fuck I tell him to do!"

My mouth dropped open. I couldn't believe what he was saying. Although part of me wanted to hate Pelmington for what he'd done to my career, I couldn't because I knew my decisions were what started it all. In my mind, he was still a great attorney who I would have jumped at another opportunity to work for. I saw him as someone who believed in the law as much as I did. Now Luke was telling me that they were working together?

"He's not as crystal clean as you believe him to be. That crooked ass muthafucka been padding cases, stealing, and all kinds of shit. Everything that you worship him for? It's fake."

I was at a loss for words. Leaning back onto the bed, I closed my mouth and tried to wrap my mind around what Luke was saying. It just seemed so unbelievable to me when I thought about it. And it had nothing to do with Pelmington's failure. It was the failure of what he stood for in my mind that bothered me. I had faith in the things I believed, and it was devastating to find out that everything I believed in was a lie. It was like going to church for years only to find out that the preacher you listened to every Sunday and believed in was a child molester.

Sighing heavily, Luke sat down at the foot of the bed and grabbed my foot, squeezing it in his hands before placing both of my feet in his lap.

"Put your faith in me, Nell." His gentle eyes cradled mine, giving me an instantaneous peace. "At the end of the day, me and you aren't all that different. We fight for people to get what they deserve. The only difference is that your fight is in the courtroom and mine is in the streets. The quicker you start to understand that shit, the more powerful we can be."

Luke gave my leg two pats and then stood up to walk out the door.

"Wait."

Stopping abruptly, he turned around and I sat back up in the bed, knowing that it was time for me to come clean about a few things. If random people from his neighborhood could go to him for help, why couldn't I?

"I've lost all of my big clients. If… If I don't do something, I won't even be able to keep the lights on. I didn't want to tell you because I was trying to handle things on my own, but I can't handle it anymore. It's gotten too out of hand."

Dropping his head, I watched as Luke massaged the facial hair on his chin before lifting up to look back at me. I prayed that he didn't ask why I was losing the accounts. I wasn't ready to tell him that part just yet.

"Don't worry about none of it anymore."

"But I don't want any handouts! If I could just have some help finding—"

Before I could finish my sentence, Luke stepped out of the room and shut the door behind him, ending the conversation. I dropped back down on the bed and the second my head touched my pillow, a sense of relief came over me. I didn't know what Luke was planning to do to help me, but I knew he wouldn't let me fail.

Even if I didn't feel like he understood what I did, he believed in me wholeheartedly. Right then, I made the decision to do the same for him. I may not ever understand how it is to be him or do what he did, but the least I could do was give him my support and put my faith in him.

Carmella

"aaaammmmmn."

Cree cupped the back of my head as I opened my jaws wide and sucked him in, pulling his erect pole in past my tonsils. Thrusting my tongue forward, I tickled the top of his head with it while I deep-throated him, knowing it was this move that drove him insane.

"I'm about to bust," he moaned loudly, telling me what I already knew because I already felt his dick begin to contract.

I removed my lips with a loud pop and quickly pulled up, lowering myself onto him without missing a single beat. With his arms wrapped around my waist and his eyes closed, he bit down on his bottom lip and squeezed down on my flesh as I rode him hard, pulling up before slamming down, gripping him with my muscles. In these rare moments that Cree let me take control, I made the most of it, pulling every damn trick out of the bag.

"Shit," he groaned. His eyes flashed open, meeting mine, and I creamed even more when I saw the desire in them.

Lifting me up, he began to control the motion, holding me in place as he slammed his dick back and forth between my walls. My head dropped back and my mouth flung open as I felt my orgasm creeping up from my toes. Cree's hands lowered down and he tugged my legs forward so I was sitting down on him, and then pulled up so that I was on my back with my legs in the air and he was kneeling down below me.

Before I could even get my bearings, he started slamming into me hard, fucking me like it was his last time. Bending down, he kept the motion going as he bit down hard on one of my nipples, doing the rough shit that I loved. He grabbed my wrists in one hand and pulled them up above my head, using the one hand that was still on my hips to brace himself as he bucked inside me like he was searching for something he'd lost.

He smacked me hard on my ass and I screamed, but God knows the last thing I wanted was for him to stop. Lowering my legs so that my feet were flat on the bed, I fucked him back, eager to make him feel the same way that he was making me.

"Stop… fuckin'… movin'… Mel!" Cree was losing control, talking through gritted teeth. I knew exactly what I was doing so I didn't stop, if anything I fucked him back even harder, contracting my pussy muscles like a pro.

"I… said… stop!"

Grabbing me by the throat, he squeezed so hard that my mouth flung open and my eyes bugged. It felt like I was floating and the sensation of my impending orgasm intensified to levels that my body could barely comprehend. I came hard, screaming loud in a high-pitch tone that only bats could hear.

Cree didn't stop until I was coming down from my high. Flinging himself back, he pulled himself from me and released on my stomach, covering my flat abs with his juices.

"I almost thought you weren't going to be able to stop yourself," I told him while yawning and stretching my naked body out on the bed. We had just woken up but after what he'd just put on me, I was more than ready to take my ass back to sleep.

"Naw. I don't want no kids," Cree replied, slapping me on the ass before giving it a little squeeze.

He stood and stretched his long, lean, and muscular body out, giving me an eyeful in the process. *My god* he was a sexy man. And what made Cree even sexier than you could see with your eyes is the fact that he didn't seem to even know how sexy he was. It was effortless to him… like looking so good came natural without him even thinking about it. Almost like he woke up in the morning, threw on some clothes, and then was like, "Oh shit, did I make myself sexy again?"

Sitting up on one elbow, I twisted my lips to the side, feeling like playing the devil's advocate for some reason.

"You don't want no kids? Well, what if I want some?"

Turning, he gave me a blank expression before chuckling to himself and shaking his head. "You must just wanna fight or some shit. We both know you ain't trying to have kids, Mel. Being a mother ain't in you."

Something about how he said what he said made a spark of heat ignite in my chest. What did he mean by that?

"Being a mother ain't in me? What the hell does that mean? You don't think I would make a good mother?"

Cocking his head to the side, Cree stared at me like I'd spawned another head from my neck. Then he shook his head and a weary expression fell over his face before he ran his hand over it.

"Man, you fuckin' up the mood right now."

Snaking my neck, I jumped up and got right up in Cree's face to set the record straight. No, I didn't want no kids, but he wasn't about to act like I couldn't make a good mother if I happened to change my mind.

"I don't care about no damn mood! What we *not* gon' do is act like I'm the kinda bitch who is so fuckin' selfish that I can't sit my ass down and have some fuckin' kids when I get good and ready to. Matter of fact, fuck what you heard! I *do* want to have kids because I know I'd make a damn good moth—"

Before I could finish, Cree grabbed me by my arm and twisted it so that I was facing the wall. With one swift motion, he entered me from behind while simultaneously pushing me down, forcing an arch in my back. My mouth gaped open like a fish out of water and my eyes bugged as I struggled to catch my breath when he began slamming into me from behind so hard that I was certain, had he not been holding my hips, I would've gone sailing out of the window in front of us.

"I'mma give you somethin' for that fuckin' mouth, Mel! You want some fuckin' kids?"

He paused, but I couldn't respond because he was fucking the words out of me. All I could do was grit my teeth and try to keep my knees from buckling. Reaching back, Cree slapped me hard on my ass and I screamed, the stinging sensation making my pussy thump even more.

"Answer my fuckin' question! You want a nigga to give you some kids, huh? Is that what the fuck you sayin'?"

"I—I—I—I—"

"What da fuck are you tryin' to say?!"

Cree reached forward and grabbed the ends of my hair, snatching my head back but not slowing down his pace. I felt like I was drunk, so caught up in how he was making me feel that I couldn't think... couldn't speak.

"Fuck... I'm 'bout to bust." Cree's words came out in a whisper but they were enough to bring me back to reality. Noting that he was making no attempts to slow down or pull out, my mind screamed when I realized that his crazy ass was about to teach me a lesson I wasn't ready to learn.

"N—n—n—no! Cree!"

"Huh, what was that?" he asked and I began to get frantic, trying to move away, but he had me in a firm grip that I couldn't escape from. I felt myself start to panic. I was *not* on the pill and knew damn well that I did *not* want no damn kids!

"Pull out, Cree! Pull out!"

Gripping me firmer, Cree only started fucking me harder. I felt his dick start to contract within my walls and I started moving my arms so fast that it probably looked like I was trying to climb up the damn walls.

"What?!"

"Pull out! PLEAAAAASE!"

Cree chuckled a little to himself before pumping me a few more times and then pulling out, sprinkling his seed all over my back. I was so tired and sore that I dropped down to my knees, collapsing at his feet. Satisfied that he'd proven his point, Cree walked around me into the bathroom and started the shower.

A few minutes later, he came back in the room and scooped me up, cradling me in his arms like a child, my legs wrapped around his waist. He walked right into the shower, placed my back on the wall, and then grabbed a washcloth. Still holding me up, he bathed me gently, cleaning away all of the evidence of our activities that morning. Once he finished, he held me under the water to rinse the soap off and I grabbed the washcloth from him.

"Naw, I don't need you to do that," he said and I shook my head.

"I want to… let me wash you."

He bit down on his back teeth, clenching his jaw, but he didn't say a word so I started putting my hands to work, rubbing soap over his chest. As he watched me, I noticed his expression softening. I cleaned every part of him I could reach and he watched me the entire time. When it was time for him to rinse the soap from his body, he walked under the water and pressed his lips to mine. Sucking on my lips and pushing his tongue inside of my mouth, he deepened our embrace, succeeding in taking my breath away.

"I love you." He whispered the words against my lips and my stomach flipped. He still had the same effect on me that he had from the very beginning.

"I love you more."

"Naw," was his only response.

Lying in the bed, dry, greased down with baby oil and too comfortable to move a single muscle, I was just about asleep again when Cree's voice entered my ears.

"I have to go. I'll be back later."

"Where are you goin'?" I asked him, yawning before cuddling up with a pillow.

"Just to handle some shit," he replied, his head bent as he texted on his phone.

I didn't say a word, just closed my eyes and pretended to go to sleep. As soon as the front door closed, I jumped up like my ass was on fire and started pulling on some clothes.

"BRYAN!" I yelled into the phone as soon as I saw the call had been picked up.

"Bitch, yes?" His voice was groggy and he was definitely irritated, but I didn't care. It was time to move.

"He just left. I turned on the tracking feature on his phone so I can follow his ass. You coming with me?"

"Hell yes!" he shouted, the thought of impending drama renewing his energy.

Not even thirty minutes later, I had Bryan in the car and I was following the directions on my phone that would lead me right to where Cree's sneaky ass was.

"Girl, we in the muthafuckin' hood," Bryan noted, pulling his scarf tighter around his neck. Bryan was dressed for the occasion with large dark black shades that nearly covered his entire face, a baseball cap on his head, a dark feathered scarf around his neck, and even gloves on his hands in case he needed to do some dirty work and didn't want to leave his prints behind. His ass was crazy.

"This isn't the hood," I told Bryan, rolling my eyes. "It's just not Manhattan, wit'cho uppity ass."

Turning his nose up, he didn't say a thing but pulled one side of his shades down to look over them and out the window. A few seconds later, I heard him gasp loudly before turning my way.

"Bitch, I swear I just saw a nigga wearing a Phat Farm jacket and some Girbaud jeans! All of Rainbow's finest is out here on display. Where the hell are you takin' meeeee?!"

"Shhhh!"

From what I was seeing on my phone, I was right around the corner from where Cree was, doing God knew what. But thankfully, I was about to find out too. Slowing the car down to a creep, I pressed my own shades onto my face just as we turned the corner. Bryan's new roommate had allowed us to borrow his Honda, so I was hoping that we would be able to fly under the radar.

"There is his car!" Bryan shrieked, grabbing onto my arm and nearly making me swerve into the other lane. "Pull to the side, pull to the side!"

Following his instruction, I slid to the side of the road in front of another residential building and placed the car in park.

"What now?" I asked, looking at Bryan who shrugged.

"Shit, I don't know. I guess we wait."

Fifteen minutes later, I was drumming my fingers against the steering wheel and chewing up the nails on my other hand when a door opened and I saw Cree walk outside. Beside me, Bryan's head was back, his mouth wide open as he snored loudly as if we'd been sitting there for hours.

"Bryan!" I knocked my hand against his chest to wake him up. "There he is!"

Bryan snorted awake, clutching his chest dramatically like he was dying. Ignoring him, I kept my eyes pinned on Cree, knowing that something was about to happen. I could feel it in my bones.

And I was right.

Cree walked outside of one of the apartments just as a brown-skinned chick came to the door. He turned around and spoke to her while she stood, leaning on the window pane. Squinting my eyes, I tried to figure out if I could place her face but, before I could run through my memory bank, another much smaller figure appeared next to her. It was a little boy, about Cree's complexion. He couldn't be more than maybe three or four years old. Reaching out, he grabbed at Cree, hugging his legs, and Cree bent down, scooping him up in his arms before kissing him on the cheek.

"Oh my god!" Bryan gasped, and I heard him slap his hand to his chest. "Is... do you think that's his son?"

Frowning, I didn't say a word as I continued to watch. Cree placed the boy down and reached into his pocket, pulling out a wad of money. He peeled off more than just a few bills and handed them over to the woman who said a couple words before pushing them into her bra.

"Oh hell no!" I had seen enough. Reaching out, I unlocked the door and snatched at the handle.

"Carmella, no!" Bryan yelled, and I felt his fingertips graze my shoulder, trying to stop me, but I wasn't having it.

There was no way this nigga was about to fuck me senseless and then leave me at the crib so that he could be with the next bitch. And not to mention, it looked like he had a kid! All this shit about how he didn't want children and blah, blah, blah, but he'd already had one that he was hiding. Hell to the fuck no, this was not about to happen. Not on my watch.

"CREE!"

Cree turned around, his face in a full frown and his eyes tight when they landed on me. He didn't even seem surprised! It was like his lying ass knew that one day his sins would come to the light.

"Who the fuck is this bitch?!" I screamed, pointing at the woman who was still standing in the doorway, the little boy who had been at her legs now in her arms.

"Mel, what da fuck are you doin' here? And lower ya fuckin' voice!"

My neck snapped back. "Lower my voice? The last thing your grimy, cheatin', nasty dick ass needs to be worried about is my voice! Why don't you tell me about this shit that you got goin' on right here. Is that your son?"

I pointed at the little boy who was staring at me with wide eyes, more than likely trying to figure out who this crazy woman was that was attacking his daddy. Instead of answering me, Cree pressed his lips firmly together and stared back at me. He didn't have to say a word to me, the resemblance was insane. The little boy had the same eyes, a little lighter of a complexion… but he was definitely a Murray. You could even see it in the way that he glared at me as he sat in his mother's arms. This was Cree's son.

"Mel, get your ass back in the car and go. I'll meet you at the house."

Tears came to my eyes and started to fall immediately. "Just tell me the fuckin' truth! You at least owe me that, Cree!"

I felt someone step up beside me and knew it was Bryan when I felt him wrap his arm around me, pulling me close to him as I continued to cry. This wasn't even like me. I didn't cry about shit but, in this moment, it was all I could do. I felt like my heart had been ripped out of my chest. Cree wasn't the man I thought he was.

"Lacey, take him inside," Cree said, addressing the woman. She gave me a long look, not an angry or gloating one—it was more curious than anything else—and then she stepped inside and closed the door.

"Bryan, do me a favor and take her ass home… Now!"

Bryan jumped about ten feet in the air before scurrying over to me and clamping his hand around my arms.

"I'm not going anywhere!" I screamed, pulling away from Bryan and stepping squarely in front of Cree to make him look at me. "You got another woman pregnant… you have a son that you didn't tell me about and you're giving her money?! Are—are you still sleeping with her?"

Cree's body went rigid and he gave me a steely look, his eyes appearing so cold, I thought I could feel ice sliding down my spine.

"I'm *not* sleepin' with her, Mel. Now I'mma tell you one mo' fuckin' time. Go home!"

Bryan tried to grab me but I ripped my arm out of his grasp again and before I knew it, I'd lunged at Cree and was pelting him with punches, hitting him everywhere that I could. Never before had I ever put my hands on a man, but never before had I been hurt in this way. For me to give my all to a man, fully let my guard down, and then for him to do this to me... I just couldn't take it. In this moment, I felt I could identify with Faviola and how she must have felt before she took her own life. Except I didn't want to hurt me, I wanted to hurt him. I wanted him to feel the same way I did.

"I *knew* you would cheat on me! I knew it! You're just like all the others... I hate you!"

It didn't take long for Cree to pin my arms behind me so that I couldn't move, but by the time he did, he had a long bloody cut down the side of his face. Gripping my body between his arms, he shook me so hard that my head bobbled back and forth like a ragdoll.

"I told you to take your stupid ass home, Carmella!"

By the time he stopped shaking me, I was too dizzy to stand on my own feet. It didn't matter to Cree because he wasn't planning on letting me walk anyways. Still holding on to me, he stomped across the street, over to the car that I'd been in with Bryan, and then opened the driver's door. I heard him press a button and the trunk clicked open. Walking around the back of the car, Cree tossed my ass right in the trunk like a bag of bricks, and I screamed bloody murder when my head hit something hard. The last thing I saw was Cree frowning down on me with absolute disgust and anger before he closed the trunk on me. Then there was darkness.

"Bryan, take her stupid ass home!" I heard Cree say, to which Bryan responded with a hasty 'mmhm'.

Folding up into fetal position, I tucked my head down, chin to chest, and cried the entire way back to the home that I shared with Cree. Everything had been so perfect, but I knew it wouldn't last, because it never did. Not for me anyways. Never before had I been able to be happy because no matter how pretty I made myself with make-up, how much I stayed in the gym to keep my hot body, or how much I showed out in the bedroom, I was always cheated on. It was like I could do anything in my power to keep a man and he'd always show me that I wasn't enough. Cree seemed to be different, but I just knew he couldn't be because all men were the same once they got comfortable. I just needed some kind of proof of what I'd already known to be true.

And this was the exact kind of proof that I'd needed.

Sidney

"*Y*ou need to clean this shit up, Sid! I don't like livin' in a fuckin' pigsty. Would it hurt you to pick up behind yourself sometimes?"

Blinking, I opened my sleepy eyes to the image of Yolo angrily tossing some clothes I'd left on the floor in a big black garbage bag. I frowned and sat up to wipe the sleep out of my eyes, hoping that whatever was about to happen wouldn't turn into an argument. I wasn't the cleanest person in the world, and we both knew that. In fact, Yolo and I joked about it often. As you probably expected, Yolo, on the other hand, was a neat freak. He was actually a little obsessive about it. Everything in his closet was organized by color, his shoes were neatly placed in order of brand, even his underwear and sock drawer was arranged according to style and color.

"I'm sorry… I was tired after I got in last night," I apologized and stood up to help him clean. I had only managed to stuff my feet into my Ugg slippers when Yolo was standing in my face, dangling a white towel that had been smeared with what looked like clown paint. Unlike regular people, Yolo only bought white towels to bathe with. That was it.

"And what the fuck is this shit?"

Rolling my eyes, I snatched it from his hands. "This is my towel that I used to wash my face! You know all that shit you make me wear so that I can look girly? All that make-up and shit? It has to come off at some point!"

"You need to figure somethin' else out then because I don't want that shit stainin' my fuckin' towels!"

I placed my hands on my hips and glared at him.

"Yolo, are you goin' to tell me what the fuck is really wrong? Because I know you aren't up this time of the morning, trippin' on me about this dumb shit!"

With my eyes on him, I waited patiently for him to respond with something good. The past few days, he'd been tripping on me for all kinds of random reasons, but I knew that it wasn't me he was pissed at. He was on edge about something and I'd been giving him time to tell me but he hadn't said a word yet.

"Ain't shit wrong with me, Sid," he said in a low voice but couldn't meet my eyes. His ass was lying.

I grabbed the basketball out of the corner of the room and tossed it at him. It hit him square in the chest but he caught it.

"One on one. I win and you have to tell me what's going on. And don't lie and say it's nothing. I know you better than that."

He knew I was right and it was all in his face even though he was trying hard to keep his composure. Somewhere between the worry lines in his forehead, the way his jaw remained clenched and the sad droop of his eyes, I could tell that something was bothering him and it was something major because he'd really been trying to hide it. Even now he was still trying.

"I'm not in the mood to play. But we do need to talk." He paused and looked down, away from my eyes, and frowned deeply at whatever it was he was thinking about. "I can't do it right now but tonight—tonight, we'll talk. Okay?"

I nodded my head and tried to ignore the feeling of impending doom that was coming over me. I had a feeling that my life was about to change once he told me whatever it was he was holding, and I wasn't sure it would be for the better. Yolo dropped the basketball to the floor and it rolled until it came to a stop at my toes. From the day we'd first met, every huge fight or issue we'd had was settled with a game of basketball, even the more serious of situations. What in the world was going on that couldn't be dealt with in our normal way?

***

"Honey, listen, I know you're supposed to come over to cook this morning but don't bother. I'm goin' to be out, okay? I'm walking out the door right now."

"Yes, Mama," I replied into the phone before dropping into the seat of my car. Normally, I would protest or ask questions to make sure she wasn't trying something slick, but I didn't even have the energy today.

"I'll see you tomorrow, okay?"

"Okay, Mama."

Hanging up the phone, I sighed and turned the key in the ignition so that I could head on to work. I would arrive much earlier than I needed to be there but I could use the extra time to clear my mind. As soon as I pulled off onto the road, my phone rang and I answered it quickly when I saw it was Carmella. I hadn't talked to her in a while and it was crazy how things had switched. It seemed I was closer to Janelle now than I was to her.

"What's up, Mel?"

"Sidney, this isn't Carmella, this is Bryan. We are here in front of Cree's grandmother's house and I'm trying to convince her to—Shit! Bitch, that hurt! You nearly wiped off my damn eyebrows! Hold on, Sidney."

There was some tussling on the other line like they were fighting or something and then Bryan came back on the line.

"Listen, I couldn't reach Janelle so I called you. I need you to help me convince this crazy ass girl not to confront this man's grandmother with her foolishness."

Carmella's voice came in on the other line, a little muffled but clear enough for me to make out every word.

"No! His ass played me for a muthafuckin' fool, had a baby on me and then didn't want to come home last night! I *know* his ass is somewhere hiding with that bitch and since I can't find their asses, I'm about to run up in here and let this God-fearing woman know—"

Pulling the phone away, I ran my hand over my forehead and sighed heavily. Faviola was gone—God bless her soul—but it seemed like I was still being pulled into the same ole drama.

"Where are you now?"

"We are in Brooklyn, in front of his grandmother's house now, right smack in the hood! And, girl, when I tell you I know I already heard some gunshots and saw a nigga throwing up gang signs—"

I rolled my eyes and couldn't help but smile. I didn't know Bryan all that well, but I did know that his ass was overly dramatic.

"I'm on my way over there now. But his grandmother just called me and said she wasn't even home so everything should be fine."

"She *is* home," Bryan informed me, breathing hard as if he were still struggling with Carmella. "I saw her in there myself. And she has somebody with her so I really don't wanna be at this lady's house with this stupid shit right now."

I sucked my teeth and told Bryan to give me five minutes before hanging up the phone. I couldn't believe Grandma Murray had lied to me just so that I wouldn't come over there and cook for her. I knew she liked her seasoned food but the shit couldn't be that damn serious!

When I pulled up, I saw Bryan and Carmella standing outside. Carmella had her arms folded in front of her chest and was leaning back on her car with a stubborn expression on her face. She wasn't even dressed, wearing what appeared to be her pajama pants and a tank top with a long jacket over the top. I jumped out the car, but not before noticing there was another car in the driveway. Grandma Murray had company.

"Thank God!" Bryan turned to me, clasping his hands together in thanks. "Sidney, please tell this crazy girl that—"

As soon as Bryan's eyes were off of her, Carmella took off, running to the door.

"Fuck," I grumbled under my breath while taking off after her. I was getting too old for this shit. At some point in my life, I needed to be able to make friends who weren't always dragging me into their relationship problems.

By the time I caught up with Carmella, she'd already rang the doorbell, knocked, and was standing in front, waiting patiently so I simply stood by her side. As determined as she was, there was nothing I could do to stop whatever was about to happen, but at least I could stick around to deal with the aftermath when Grandma Murray would use Carmella's head for batting practice and smack the shit out of her.

The front door opened and Grandma Murray emerged, her questioning eyes looking directly at Carmella. In her arms was a small boy—cute kid, appeared to be about four years old.

"You *knew*?!" Carmella gasped, looking at the little boy with her mouth wide open.

"Chile, what are you—"

I stepped up and Grandma Murray's eyes went to me, widening as if she hadn't realized I'd been standing there.

"Mama, I'm sorry for disturbing you but—"

I stopped speaking when I saw the discomfort in her eyes. She looked away from me and cupped the little boy in her arms, as if protecting him... from me? There was movement behind her and I looked, shocked when I saw that it was the woman I'd seen speaking to Yolo at the club. The same one I'd seen driving by here the other day. What was she doing inside of Grandma Murray's house?

"And that's that bitch right there!" Carmella shouted. "I can't *believe* this! Who didn't know about Cree's secret child and babymama? Am I the only one?"

"Cree?" I asked, stepping up. I looked at the little boy who was staring back at me. "This is Cree's baby?"

"Yes!" Carmella answered for me. "I caught him at the bitch's house the other day! He was being a good ole secret Daddy, stopping by to take care of the mama and the baby. Gave her money and all. And now she's here! I can't believe you didn't tell me that Cree had a baby!"

The fire in Grandma Murray's eyes came alive and she flashed her beautiful hazel eyes at Carmella, curling her lip in a way that said she was about to set her straight the good ole fashioned way.

"Chile, you better hush yo' mouth before I reach in there and pull out that disrespectful tongue!" She spoke with so much grit that even Carmella, the one who didn't shut the hell up for nobody, clamped her mouth closed and bent her head down like a child being chastised.

"If you come over here pointin' fingers at someone, first you need to make sure that you know what you *think* you know. *This* is not Cree's baby, gal!"

"Ahh!" Bryan chirped, reminding me that he was still standing behind me.

Carmella's neck snatched up and her light caramel skin seemed to nearly go white. "It's not? That's not Cree's son?"

"No, he's not!" Grandma Murray answered firmly. "Lil' raggedy girl," she added for good measure.

With my brows bunched together, I stepped forward, my eyes planted on the baby boy, staring at his brown eyes and light, buttery skin. He definitely looked like he could be Cree's kid... or at least related to him.

"Well, then whose son is he?" I heard myself asking the question I was thinking to myself. My eyes went up to Grandma Murray's face, and I was concerned when I saw her lips press together in a slight grimace, as if she were scared to say. The woman still standing behind her dropped her head down, looking just as uncomfortable as Grandma Murray did and I was beginning to feel.

"Mama?" She sighed and looked at me with apologetic eyes, begging for forgiveness before I even knew why.

"He—he's Yolo's."

"Yolo?" I repeated back to her, a single tear sliding down my cheek.

"Yes, baby. I'm so sorry you had to find out this way…"

Oh god.

I staggered backwards and placed my hand to my chest. I felt like I was going to faint.

Janelle

"*U*m… Janelle, you may want to come out and see this."

Lifting my head from the pile of bills on my desk, I frowned slightly when I saw the uneasy expression on Gerald's face. Standing, I started over to him, hoping that whatever was waiting for me was something I could handle.

"What's going on?"

"We, um… we have new clients."

I smiled. "That's good news!"

The expression on Gerald's face said that he wasn't so sure, but I didn't share his worries. After looking at the bills coming in, I couldn't be picky about the money we had coming in. Turning the corner to the conference room, I almost skipped through the doors. That was just how excited I was. But I was in for a huge surprise.

Walking into the conference room, I could barely get my thoughts together before my nostrils were hit with the very distinct odor of marijuana. Inside the medium-sized room was a table where five men were sitting, waiting on me. Just one look told me that these were clients that Luke had sent me. Each man wore the finest street clothes and were smothered with jewelry, enough to probably purchase a few homes, cars, and still have enough left over to put up for a rainy day. Their skin was covered with various tattoos, markings that most likely pointed to whatever gang they were affiliated with, among other things.

At the head of the table, in the seat that was normally reserved for me—being that this was my firm and all—sat a man who was obviously the boss of the others. He was large in size, had a thick and bushy but nicely shaped full beard and probably about double the tattoos as the others, the most noticeable ones to me being the teardrops coming from his eyes and the 6-pointed star on his muscular neck.

When I walked inside of the conference room, all of their eyes turned to me, but it was the man at the head of the table who stood with his hands clasped together in front of his body.

"Are you Mrs. Murray?"

Yep… these were *definitely* friends of Luke's.

"I'm Ms. Pick—well, actually, yes, that's me. Um… how can I help you?"

Searching the room for a chair, I was just about ready to sit in the corner rather than ask any of the men to move.

"You can sit here," the boss said, pointing to a chair that was occupied by a man sitting to his right. The man stood and pulled the chair out for me. Biting the inside of my lip, I eased into the chair, thanking him when he pushed it in for me.

"We need your assistance. I'm about to make some moves… and it would be good to have an attorney on retainer," the boss began. He took a seat and pulled out a toothpick, securing it between his teeth while he spoke.

"Okay." I spoke slowly, but my mind was running, trying to figure out how I could ask the questions I was thinking in the most respectful way possible.

"May I ask what you do for a living?"

One of his men snorted out a laugh and the boss cut his eyes at him, giving him a menacing stare that silenced him instantly. I sucked in a breath and let it out slow. This was about to be an interesting meeting.

"I'm into… distribution," he said, rubbing his hands together. The edge of his upper lip curled, and I noticed that he had a full gold grill, complete with diamonds surrounding the perimeter of each tooth.

"Distribution…" I said, nodding my head. I glanced over to Gerald, who looked like he was about to die, and then dropped my head to my notebook.

"Yeah, but you don't need to write that down," the boss told me and I dropped the pen on the table like it was on fire. Watching me intently, his upper lip twitched and his eyes seemed to cloud up.

"You sure you're Outlaw's girl?"

Pressing my lips together into a thin line, I nodded my head. But when he cut his eyes to look at one of his men, I read what he was saying without speaking, and realized that I needed to get myself together. I was positive when Luke sent them my way, they weren't expecting to meet with a lawyer who was just as scared of them as anyone else. In addition to that, if I was supposed to represent them, I couldn't act like I was afraid to speak.

Channeling Luke's energy, I cleared my throat, picked up my

pen and started again. "Anything that we discuss in here is covered by attorney client privilege. Now, in order to effectively represent you and…" My eyes raked over the other men at the table. "…your team, I will need to take notes and ask questions that you'll need to answer honestly. Got it?"

The man's eyes were black as coal and when he settled them on my face, I felt like I was going to fold up and immediately turn into the coward that he surely thought I was. However, I kept my composure and stared at him with the intensity that he gave me, remembering that this was someone Luke had sent my way, so he obviously had faith in me that I could handle it.

"I got it," the man replied, an unsettling grin spreading across his lips.

Nodding, I took a deep breath and continued. "You can start with your name."

"Bone."

I gave him a pointed look. "Your real name. The one your mama gave you."

He snickered at my newfound brazenness. "Sloan Jacobs. But I prefer to be called Bone."

"Thank you, Bone. Now what exactly will you need my assistance with?"

Leaning forward, Bone folded his hands together and leaned forward on his elbows, looking me square in the eye as he explained all of the things that he needed my help with. Mainly assistance with his legitimate businesses, but he stated that should a situation arise where he'd need a criminal defense attorney, he expected me to be able to step in.

"Well, my primary work has been as a prosecuting attorney—"

"Good, then you can expect the angle they'll come at," Bone surmised easily, smirking a little as he spoke. "That's the best kind of defense. You'll be expecting their moves. Like playing chess."

Bone didn't seem like the drug dealers I'd heard about or, in rare cases, seen standing on the corners, peddling their product to whatever person approached them for a quick fix. He was well versed, conducted himself like a highly educated professional and, outside of the physical, could easily blend right in with the corporate world.

Still, there was a threatening side to him that said he wasn't one to be played with, and that's what separated him from someone like Gerald. Bone gave you the feel of a killer. No matter how comfortable you got speaking with him, you couldn't possibly forget that there was a very real possibility that he'd easily blow your brains out if you did the wrong thing.

"Okay, I can help you," I told him with a sigh. "My retainer is—"

Bone lifted his hand, cutting me off, and then signaled to one of his men. The man grabbed a duffle bag that had been sitting at his feet and pushed it across the table to me. I lifted my brow and peeked at Bone, getting his permission with a slight nod of his head before opening it up. My mouth nearly dropped to the tabletop when I saw that the bag was filled with money neatly wrapped with rubberbands.

"I think this will cover it," Bone affirmed. Standing up, he tapped the table twice with his knuckles and the other men stood as well. I guess that was his signal that the meeting had ended.

"I'll have someone forward you all the details concerning my businesses, and I'll catch up with you sometime next week about the other things."

With a tacit nod, I shook his hand and then watched as the men filed out of the conference room. I followed behind them, noting that every eye in the building was on them until they walked out of the front doors.

"So... our clientele has changed drastically," Gerald stated, standing next to me. I turned to look at him and he raised both of his brows, making me laugh a little.

"Sure has. You're good with that?"

Scoffing, he nodded. "Damn right. I go where the money is. And if anyone else here has a problem with it, they can be replaced."

It felt good to know that Gerald's loyalty was exactly where I needed it to be. It made me feel like maybe I could trust him to help me with something else. Grabbing his arm, I walked into my office and closed the door behind us.

"Gerald, I have to ask you something." My nerves took over and I started winding my hands together. "I know that our other clients pulled out because a video surfaced..." Gerald averted his eyes away from my face and cleared his throat. "...I know who the person is who sent it. It's my old roommate. I just need help finding her."

Among Gerald's many skills, he was also our investigator. If anyone could find out where Val was, it was him.

"I'm on it. Give me a name and an hour."

Janelle

"s this it?"

The look of disgust on Sidney's face most likely mirrored mine. True to his word, Gerald was able to get an address for Val in less than an hour. I knew I didn't want to see her alone so I asked Sidney to go with me. She'd been quiet and not like herself all day. I knew it had something to do with Yolo, but she hadn't mentioned it to me yet and I didn't want to press. Still, I thought that riding with me to see Val would help get her mind off of whatever she was dealing with.

"Yeah, this matches the address Gerald gave me."

I looked at the paper in my hand to be sure before gaping back up at the building in front of me. It was an old, broken down looking house that didn't look safe enough to even live in. There was gray electric tape up to the windows, a dirty box-spring mattress on the lawn outside, and an overflowing garbage can on the side of the house that had already become an attraction for mice. I couldn't believe Val was staying here.

"This is some nasty shit." Sidney went to open the door and then snatched her arm away from the handle and screwed up her face. "You sure you need me to go in with you?"

I took in a sharp breath and shook my head. "No, I don't know where her mind is and she might not be comfortable speaking in front of someone she doesn't know. Just keep your phone on you in case I need you."

Sidney looked more relieved than a little bit to not have to follow me inside. "Will do."

Though I might have put on a brave face, I was clutching my phone in my hand so tightly that it was beginning to ache. With my jaw clenched, I walked up to the door and knocked hard and then wiped my knuckles, feeling as though I'd touched something disgusting.

"Who is it?!"

The voice definitely belonged to Val, but it seemed like she was already in a fucked up mood and she didn't even know it was me at the door. But then again, look at how she was living. It was obvious why her mood was sour. If I was her, I'd be angry all day for living in this shit too.

"It's Janelle."

"Who?"

"Janelle!"

The door snatched open and the next thing I saw was Val standing in front of me. Or… at least I *thought* it was Val. Val had always been beautiful, trendy, and particular about her appearance. She was like Carmella in that way, the difference being that Val was always throwing herself at some man who couldn't do shit for her and would stick around long after he gave her his ass to kiss.

But things had changed for Val and I could see it just from looking at her. Standing before me in a skintight, one piece, leopard print, spandex outfit that looked like it had spent about a hundred too many times in the dryer rolling around in balls of lint, I couldn't believe how far she'd fallen off. She looked like she was wearing a bird's nest for weave, sporting a style so jacked up, I could see the tracks. Her skin was dry and ashy and there was nasty shit in the corner of her eyes. And if you thought all that was bad, you wouldn't believe how she *smelled*. I'll give you a hint: Old pampers.

"Val?"

"The fuck you doin' here?!" she spat and then in the next second she was laughing with her index finger in the air, shaking it at me. "Ohhh, I know why you're here. If you're going to ask me to delete that video, you can forget about it. I'm saving it just in case you have any other big money clients who may want to see it."

"Why would you want to do that to me? I haven't done anything to deserve—"

Tossing her head back, she started to laugh… or I should say cackle, because that's closer to how it sounded.

"Of course you wouldn't think you did anything to deserve the bad shit that happens in your life. You never do! In your mind, your shit didn't stink. You always thought you were better than me, lecturing me on everything you thought I was doing wrong. Flaunting your daddy's money in my face and bragging about your nice new job while looking down on me for not knowing what I wanted to do with my life."

My lips parted but I wasn't sure how to respond. Honestly, I didn't know Val felt that way about me and I didn't understand why she did. Yes, I gave her my opinion on the decisions she made but I was trying to help.

"Val… I never flaunted anything in front of you! We lived in the same low rent apartment in Brooklyn because that's all we could afford and only if we put our money together. And I was happy about my job, of course, but I never bragged about it. The only reason I ever gave my opinion on your life was because I saw you like a sister… I do the same to them."

Sucking her teeth, she folded her arms and then rolled her eyes. "Well, what about Outlaw? How do you explain the way you took him from me? I could be the one living the good life, riding around in a Benz and living in a big ole house if *you* hadn't stole him from me!"

It was crazy how, over time, the mind changed reality into whatever the hell you wanted to imagine it to be. She really thought that if I wasn't standing in the way, she would be living my life.

"Val, you're not with Luke because he didn't want you. The decision he made had nothing to do with me! And, yes, while it may be against some kind of roommate rule for me to get with him after you went on a date with him, the fact of the matter is even if I were not around, he wouldn't have stayed with you!"

"How do you know that?" she screamed, her eyes tearing up. It was then that I realized how much she really blamed me for her situation. As insane as it seemed to me, she really believed that I'd stolen her life.

"Val, think about it… you met him, he took you out, and then did you forget what you told me happened when y'all came back?"

Her eyes narrowed and she scratched at her cheek, leaving white ashy lines behind.

"Let me help you out," I continued. "You said that you tried to have sex with him but he wasn't into it. You told me that he left after telling you that you were a nice girl but he didn't want to try anything with you."

Her eyes seemed to cloud over for a short while and then her expression softened a little. I could see that I was getting through to her, but I wasn't sure it would be enough to make amends. People like Val were too used to blaming everyone else for their problems. It was never their fault when they got in bad situations; it was always someone else's. As much as she seemed to think that way about me, it was something she dealt with too.

"I don't hate you, Val. I never did. I thought we were friends until what happened at the party. I just didn't expect for you to sit there and allow something bad to happen to me."

Bringing up that incident must have been a sore spot for Val because, in the next second, she was crying real tears, bawling as if she found out that someone close to her had died.

"That was the worst day of my life! You don't know... you don't know what he did to me! And it was all because of you."

Pursing my lips, I tilted my head to the side, trying to catch her eyes. "What *who* did to you?"

"Outlaw."

Now I was the one confused about how things had ended because the last thing I knew, the only thing Luke did to her was end the party that she'd thrown in our apartment and demand that she cleaned up the mess. From what I knew, he'd never come into contact with her again.

"The day you kicked me out, I had nowhere to go. After I packed all of my things, I was driving around, looking for a cheap place to stay when I saw him and some other guys standing on the curb, talking. I was desperate… you know my family ain't shit! After everything that went down, I realized the only person I had out here was you, but I'd already fucked that up. So, I went to Outlaw and asked him to speak to you and plead my case so you'd let me stay." She paused and licked her lips, trembling a little before she continued. "H—he told me to go to an address and ask for a nigga named 'Scooter' and said he'd look out for me. Scooter was a fuckin' pimp!"

My thoughts merged once it became obvious what Val was saying. In an instance, everything I felt about her and what she'd almost allowed to happen to me—all of those bad thoughts I'd been holding in—none of it mattered anymore.

"I know it was stupid but I didn't know what else to do… I told myself that I'd had sex before. It wasn't like I was a virgin. And… I'd definitely done it with men who didn't deserve me so what was the difference?" She grabbed the neck of her one piece and used it to blow her nose. "After a few times, I realized it was a trap. I never saw any of the money. It all went to Scooter and then he'd buy the things I needed. I tried to tell him I was done and threatened to leave, but Scooter beat me up so bad that I stayed in the hospital for a whole week. When they discharged me, he was the one who picked me up… holding flowers. It was then that I realized Scooter would never let me go."

I blinked away the tears that were in my eyes and reached out to touch her on the shoulder, hoping it would bring some comfort.

"Are you still working for Scooter?" I asked her and she nodded her head.

"When he calls me on the cell, it means it's time to work. If I don't answer, it could be bad for me. Really bad."

My shoulders drooped and I dropped my head low. All of this was on me. No, I hadn't been the one to hand her over to Scooter, but the series of events that landed her there had been put in motion by me.

"I'll fix this," I told her. "If you don't want to work with Scooter anymore, I promise you don't have to."

Val's brows furrowed and her bottom lip trembled. "B—but what will I do? This house… everything I have belongs to Scooter. He pays for it with the money that—"

"Don't worry about any of that. I'll make sure you're given the fair chance you deserve," I said, and I meant every word. If it was the last thing I did, I would get Val out of the situation she was in. We'd both made stupid mistakes but there was no way that I could leave her like this. My heart couldn't take it.

Val's eyes brightened and she looked at me in awe. "After everything I've done, you'll still help me?"

I nodded my head. "I don't care about all of that right now. Just grab anything that you don't want to leave behind and get in the car with me. I'll take you to a hotel and get you checked in there until we can figure out our next move. I just really don't want you to be here where Scooter can find you. I have to get you out of here."

At the mention of Scooter, Val's face seemed to pale and her shoulders went tight. Looking at her, I wondered what kind of horrible, terrible things Scooter had to do to her in order for her to become afraid just at the mention of his name.

"I—I just need the night to get my affairs in order." Val licked her lips and took a couple steps back. Her eyes were darting everywhere around us, anywhere but in my face. Something had happened. Just that quick, I'd lost her.

"Huh?"

"Just give me tonight to pack up a few things and get myself together." She forced a smile on her lips. "I'll be ready for you when you come back."

I frowned, feeling like something was off.

"Okay," I agreed, even though I felt like I should have said more to encourage her to leave. "I'll be back over here tomorrow around this same time. That work for you?"

Val nodded her head and pulled me into a hug, wrapping her arms around me so tightly that I could barely breathe.

"Thank you so much, Janelle. After everything I've done, I can't believe you'd still look out for me. You truly are the better person."

Wiping away the tears from my eyes, I turned around and headed back to my car, feeling satisfied that I'd done something to change someone's life for the better. As soon as I got home, I called Luke and told him everything, about the video, about Val, and I told him that I wanted to help her. I told him that I wanted him to get her a place and give her some money so she could start fresh. He promised to talk to Scooter and promised to set her up with a new apartment and some money so that she could look out for herself.

But things didn't work out quite in my favor. By the time Luke had called Scooter, it was too late. Val had already told him that she was leaving and he'd already made good on his word. He'd told her that she wouldn't leave him unless it was in a body bag and that was exactly what happened.

The next day when Luke called Scooter to tell him to let Val go, she was already dead.

Luke

"Yo, this marriage shit is crazy as hell."

Pulling off my fitted cap, I dropped it on the top of the table and sat down next to Cree who seemed like he was in his own thoughts, sipping from a red cup. Cree was always the most laid back muthafucka in the room because his ass was always drinking on something Yolo made to mellow him out. I could use some of whatever he had because at the moment, I was stressed as hell.

"Nigga, you ain't even married yet," Kane reminded me, chuckling a little as he lit up a cigar.

"Well, I fuckin' feel like it." I ran my hand over my face and let out a weary breath.

Honestly, I didn't feel guilty at all about sending Janelle's ex-roommate to Scooter because, had she had her way, Janelle would've probably been gang-raped in front of a group of people just because she was on some jealous shit. Not to mention the fact that, even though I sent her to Scooter, she was the one who made the decision to stay and do business with him.

On top of that, after Janelle tried to help her ass, it seemed to me that she didn't really want it. Why else would she call that nigga, baiting him by telling him that she was leaving? I really felt like, deep down, she didn't want to be saved. There was no other explanation for it and that's what I told Janelle. She didn't seem to blame me for any of it, but I could tell that it affected her in some way that she didn't want to talk about. What fucked me up was that I couldn't do anything to help her.

"Where the hell is Yolo's stupid ass?" I asked, noting that he was the only one missing.

"Probably somewhere in denial," Cree answered with a shrug.

I lifted my brows. "He still tryin' to act like the kid ain't his? You confirmed it, right?"

Cree nodded his head. "Anybody lookin' at the lil' muthafucka can tell he's a Murray. Yolo just needs to man up and take the blood test. That nigga is trippin.'"

At that exact moment, the door behind me opened and Yolo walked in, looking crazy in the face like he hadn't slept in days. The crazy part of it was, even though he was obviously stressed to the max, this nigga still managed to be dressed fly as hell, matching from his headband to his shoelaces.

"Pretty ass nigga, you can manage to dress up in all this fancy shit but you can't answer yo' phone, huh?" Kane said, obviously noticing the same thing I had.

With his head low, Yolo slid into a chair next to Tank. "Ain't felt like talkin.'"

"Why?" I asked him, frowning. "Because you found out you got a kid? Nigga, you on some stupid shit right now. I'd expect this kinda shit from Kane—" Kane shot me a crazy look. "—but not from you. You always wanted a son and now you got one... da fuck wrong with you?"

Jumping up, Yolo slammed his fist against the table.

"That's the shit that's pissing me the fuck off!" Yolo snapped. "I *always* wanted a son. Out of us all, I'm the nigga who *always* wanted a kid. And then I find out that I had one all this time but this bitch hid him from me so that she could pretend he belonged to another muthafucka. The only reason she decided to tell me the truth was because the nigga she was pretending was his daddy was killed last year!"

"But my nigga, that ain't no reason to avoid your seed," I argued with him. "I get that you mad and shit but you can't keep actin' like shorty don't exist."

Yolo sat down and dropped his head on the table, covering it with his arms. "I'm not avoidin' him. I'm just tryin' to get my head around this shit so I don't fuckin' kill this chick." Raising his head up, he ran his hand over his face in distress. "I missed out on the first few years of his life because she was on some bullshit."

"At least it wasn't because of some fucked up decisions you made." Kane shook his head, thinking about how he'd been robbed of his daughter's first few years. But not because of Teema, the blame for that shit rested solely on him.

"How Sid takin' it?" I asked, and Yolo let out a heavy sigh.

"I haven't seen her."

"Damn, nigga, you avoidin' her too?" I frowned, staring at my older brother.

Of all of us, Yolo was the most sensitive and he took everything to heart. But in this case right here, he needed to man the fuck up. I wouldn't be in my right state of mind either had something like this happened to me, but ain't no point in running from the shit.

"I was gonna talk to her about it but she found out before I could. The kid was at Big Mama's house and she saw him. Big Mama told her that he was my son." He ran a finger over the top of his lip pensively. "The past few days I been goin' off on her about silly shit... leavin' her clothes on the floor, bein' messy... dumb stuff that I was only mad about because I was pissed off and didn't know how to tell her about the kid."

Shaking my head, I scratched at my jaw.

"Naw, nigga, y'all just been together too long. That wasn't because you was stressin'. After you been with someone for a minute, little shit that they do start fuckin' with you. The other day, I was eating a grape and Janelle looked like she was about to slap the shit out of my ass, talkin' about I was smacking. When we first got together, the shit didn't even bother her. Now she 'bout to kill a nigga. She was ready to body my ass... over a *fuckin'* grape."

"Naw, crazy just runs in their family, bruh," Tank added, speaking up for the first time since I walked in the door. With a sly grin, I placed my attention on him. I'd forgotten he was dating Janelle's little sister.

"That's right, you datin' ole girl... what's her name?"

"Mixie," Tank replied with a groan. "And she drivin' my ass crazy. All my life I've been playin' the field, never wanted to settle down. Now I decide to settle down and it's the chick who don't wanna be tied down. What type of shit is that?" He held his hands out, palms up.

I screwed my face up at what he was saying. I had to get some clarity on a few things.

"Wait... so she with you, but she fuckin' other niggas?"

Tank's eyes went dark and he shook his head, his hands tightening into fists. "She better not be fuckin' another nigga if she don't want me to cancel his ass. Mixie know better than that shit... she just don't want to commit to nothing. It's fucked up."

"That's karma comin' for your ass," Cree chimed in, still sipping.

"Karma? Ain't that yo' chick?" Tank's dumb ass asked with a confused look on his face.

"Nigga, I said 'karma' not Carmella," Cree clarified, laughing at Tank. "Karma is coming for you... you fucked around on these hoes for so long and now you wanna get it straight with somebody but she done flipped the script on you."

Sitting back in his seat, Tank folded his arms across his chest and sulked while we all laughed at him. Even Yolo managed to let out a few chuckles. It was crazy how shit turned on him. I knew it would one day.

"She might be the one to break your heart, you poutin' ass nigga," I joked, knowing that I was only pissing Tank off. I had to deal with the jokes when I was actin' all soft for Janelle, so I wasn't handing out no mercy with this shit.

"Well, I ain't got y'all nigga's problems." Cree pulled the headphones from his ears and sat them on the table. "Ever since Carmella found out that Yolo's kid wasn't mine, she been blessin' ya boy properly day and night. That guilt been eatin' at her. Got her treatin' a nigga like a king."

I cut my eyes at Cree and the stupid looking grin on his face.

"Shut up, wit'cho gloatin' ass."

After talking for a while, Kane cleared his throat and we all went quiet, prepared to discuss business. After laying low for a while, every one of us was ready to get back to business. And with Pelmington no longer a concern, the sky was the limit for what we could do. Out of everybody, I was probably the most hype about getting back in work mode.

Sitting at home or sitting on the block all day wasn't for me. Even though my money was invested in ways that constantly had me making money, there was nothing like the feeling a nigga got from working hard for what he earned. Not to mention, I was more than ready to shoot some shit up.

"Outlaw, how we lookin' on weapons?"

I leaned forward and nodded. "Yeah, I got the order coming in from Bone and his crew. They got some new shit I wanna try out."

"Diamond embedded bulletproof vests?" Cree joked.

"Fuck you, nigga," I shot back with a chuckle. "But, for real, how the hell you know 'bout them?"

Tank almost choked, laughing. "I know yo' flashy ass didn't get no shit like that Outlaw. That is bogus, even for you."

Thinking, I ran a finger over my top lip. "Naw, he ain't have nothing like that. But shit… that kinda sound fly as fuck."

"This nigga want a bedazzled bulletproof vest. I done heard it all!" Obviously, Tank was having the time of his life, laughing at my expense.

"If you get one, I want one too," Yolo said with a grin.

"I'll grab you one to match every outfit. I know how yo' ass roll."

"Y'all wildin," Kane cut in but he couldn't even hide the smirk on his face. "The day niggas start wearing bedazzled vests is the day I get out the game."

"It ain't bedazzled, it's diamonds, bruh," I corrected, setting the record straight. "Try me again with that soft shit and I'll beat ya ass, Kane." I playfully lifted my fist at him.

Kane's smirk only grew on his face. "It's been a long time since I put my foot in ya ass, Outlaw. We can go when you ready."

"Naw, nigga, you tell me when you ready."

Shaking his head, Kane chuckled before falling back into checking the details for our next job. We had a while before we were going to be ready to make a move because I wasn't going anywhere until Janelle had the baby, but we always planned well in advance. 'If you failed to plan, you planned to fail,' something we lived by.

"Aye, Yolo, let me holla at you, bruh."

The meeting was over, all details were squared away, and everybody was going their separate ways but I needed to handle some business with my brother for a minute. I didn't know what it was about me and kids, but I couldn't sit by and let any of my brothers treat theirs wrong. It was the same way when it came to Kane and his daughter; when he turned his back, I was there, calling Kenya to check on her, visiting her, and giving Teema money even though she never asked. Now that I knew Yolo had a son, there was no way I was going to let him not be a father. Even Tank managed to be a decent father to all his damn kids, so there was no way Yolo's ass was about to use a stupid ass excuse to not see his son. Not on my watch.

Maybe it was because of the way I saw family; it was well known that I'd die for mine, no questions asked. If someone was blood, they could always count on me to go hard for them. That's one of the main reasons I'd been so cautious about having kids. Once I brought a life into the world, I knew that there was nothing on Earth that would stop me if someone wronged them. Imagine if I'd gotten one of those raggedy ass hoes I used to fuck with pregnant and she tried to play me because she had my daughter. Or if she tried to keep my child from me or treated her wrong. There wasn't a damn thing anyone could say to stop me from killing her ass.

"What's up, man?" Yolo had a straight expression on his face but I could tell from the look in his eyes that he knew what was up.

"I need you to ride with me for a minute," I told him, and he nodded his head without saying a word.

The entire way over to Yolo's babymama's house, a chick named Lacey according to Cree, Yolo was quiet as hell and I didn't try to strike up conversation with him either. I knew that he had to be deep in his thoughts, trying to get his mind right before he saw his son. I couldn't blame him for being mad because I would be too.

Thinking about how old the little boy was, if she had told Yolo about him, he wouldn't have ever gotten back with his crazy ass ex, and she wouldn't have gotten pregnant and then killed their child. There was a lot that wouldn't have ever happened if she'd given him the opportunity for him to be a father. If it were me, I'd round up some of these roughneck hoes in the hood and pay them to beat her ass one good time. Yeah, I was trying to be mature and shit now that I was on my grown man and had a young one on the way, but I would've done it anyways.

"You gon' be alright if we go in there?" I asked Yolo once we were in front of Lacey's house. "I'm not gon' have to pull you from off her ass, am I?"

Sighing heavily, Yolo pulled off his fitted cap and shook his head. "I'm not gon' touch that bi—that girl."

I nodded my head but made no moves to get out the car yet because it seemed like Yolo might need a few more minutes to collect himself.

"It's just fucked up, you know what I mean?" Yolo let out a tense chuckle. "I mean, I know he only three, but I'm scared as hell to see that lil' boy, bruh. I never thought I'd look in my son's eyes and he not recognize me as his father. For his whole life, she been teaching him to call some other nigga 'Daddy' and now here I am... what the hell he supposed to call me? I ain't shit to him!"

I shook my head, hearing what he was saying, but knowing he was wrong. "Naw, I see where you're coming from, fam, but it ain't like that. I won't lie and say shit won't be awkward or that his lil' ass won't be lookin' at you funny style at first... but it ain't like he's thirteen or some shit. Imagine if his ass was older and you walked up talkin' about 'call me Daddy'? You'd have to beat his ass like a grown man before he'd accept that shit. He's only three. Give him some candy and he'll be callin' you Daddy, Mama, Barney, or whatever else the hell you tell him to."

Turning, Yolo gave me a bug-eyed look and then fell out laughing. "Nigga, I can always count on you to say some off the wall shit. You ain't got 'em all, Outlaw."

I half-smirked and shrugged. Something caught my eye ahead of us and when I looked up, I saw that Lacey had opened up the front door and was standing at the entrance, staring at us. I turned to Yolo and noticed that he had his eyes on her too.

"Let's do this shit."

I hung back a little and allowed Yolo to walk forward and address Lacey while I texted Janelle to check on how she was doing and tell her I loved her. Situations like these made me thank God that He saw fit to bless my ass like he did. After all the shit I'd done in my life, I really ain't deserve nobody like her but He gave her to me anyways. I would show my gratitude by treating her right until my dying day.

"Aye, Outlaw, you comin' in?" Yolo asked, making me lift my head. I took a good look at my brother and then shook my head once I was sure that he wouldn't end up two-piecing Lacey if I left him alone.

"Naw, I'll let you have yo' privacy. I'll meet lil' man after you're done."

Yolo nodded his head and walked inside, closing the door behind him. Dropping my head again, I checked my phone but Janelle hadn't responded. I knew that she was busy these days but I hoped that was the reason she hadn't replied and it wasn't because she actually blamed me for what happened to her friend. Even though she said she didn't, I knew the situation hit her hard.

"Outlaw, is that you?"

I glanced ahead of me and almost had to do a double-take when I saw it was Briyana walking towards me, looking about a million times better than she had the other night.

"What's up, Bri-Bri?" I greeted her, making her smile hard when I used the nickname we'd given her in our younger days.

"I'm good. Thanks to you." She walked over and hugged me tight, pressing her body to mine. I pulled back and leaned against the car, a smile on my lips because I knew her young ass was on some bullshit.

For the longest, Briyana had been trying to get my attention and persuade me to fuck with her on a sexual level. I'd never made a move because her brother was my homeboy and I knew, if I had a sister, I'd beat any nigga's ass if he messed her over. Still, I always had to admit that shawty had a bangin' ass body.

"What you doin' over here?" Her eyes went to Lacey's apartment door and she frowned slightly before looking back to me. "You comin' to see her?"

I simply nodded my head. It was obvious she was feeling some kind of way, thinking that I was visiting another chick, but it wasn't my job to ease her thoughts. She wasn't my girl and I ain't owe her shit.

"Aye, tell Pops I said 'what up?' a'ight?" It was my way of politely dismissing her but Briyana didn't get it.

"You can always come by and tell him yourself," she started and then licked her lips. "You know, he always thought you and I would end up together."

I knew that shit was a lie but I didn't tell her. Pops had always thanked me for being like a brother to Briyana and like a son to him, something he wouldn't have said if he were trying to pair us up.

"Oh yeah?" I replied, looking at the screen of my phone again. Still nothing from Janelle.

"Yeah… what 'bout you? Do you think we can make something happen?"

Chuckling, I cut my eyes from her and ran my hand over my jawline. "Listen, you know I'm engaged, right? You met my fiancé the morning that I drove you and Pops home. Remember?"

Scoffing, she rolled her eyes and giggled a little. "Duh, I already know that. I don't mind sharing. You're too much for one woman. Niggas ain't stickin' with one bitch no more."

"Word?" I replied with my brows lifted.

She rolled her eyes again. "Duh!"

I chuckled again and shook my head. Chicks these days made it too easy for niggas to mutt they asses. Briyana was spoiled goods in my opinion, thanks to Remy selling her pussy to niggas with no standards, but she still was a beautiful girl and could have a future if she tried her hand at it. Her mind was fucked though. For her to even think that she could be a decent replacement for Janelle let me know that.

When I first met Janelle, she wouldn't even let me make her ass ride in the backseat. That was one of the first things that proved to me that she wasn't just any other woman I'd messed with. She demanded better from me and it ended up making me a better man because she wouldn't accept anything less.

You fuck around with chicks in the slums and you end up slumming it right with them. Since they don't want better for themselves, they don't expect better from you. And for most niggas, the easier you make shit for them, the less they work for anything more because they don't have to. Then they'll look up, ten years later and they'll still be doing the same shit; stuck selling dime bags on the corner or calling another nigga 'bossman' all because they didn't get with a woman who was worth anything.

My pops always said that a man was the head of the household but the woman was the neck and the head couldn't do shit without the neck. I always clowned him for that when I was younger and dumber, telling my brothers that, in other words, he was sayin' that he'd given our moms his balls. But now I was seeing that what he was saying was true.

Before Janelle, I had nothing to live for. I was reckless because I didn't give a damn about whether or not I got to see the next day. Now everything had changed and I was making future plans, investing my money, thinking about the consequences before I did crazy shit, and stacking my bread so that my daughter could buy anything her little ass could dream of.

"So what's it gonna be?" Briyana asked me, cocking her head to the side. I was about to answer when my phone chimed in my hand, grabbing my attention.

Janelle: I love you too. Sorry, was on a call with Bone. He's kinda scary but I'm thuggin' it out though.

"My baby thug," I said to myself, smiling hard at Janelle's innocent ass claiming to be a 'thug.' She wouldn't last two seconds in the hood.

"Huh?"

I looked up, remembering that Briyana was standing there waiting for me to agree to something that wasn't going to ever happen.

"Naw," I replied, shaking my head. "I'm not about that life you tryin' to get into. I'm a one woman man."

Smiling, she tilted her head. "You serious?"

"As a heart attack. I'll holla at you later. Stay sweet, a'ight?" I didn't wait for a response before walking around to the other side of the car and hopping on top of the trunk. Briyana, not too happy about being dismissed so easily, followed me around the car and stood in front of me, a persistent expression on her face. I'd been trying to play it nice with her out of respect, but I could see that I was going to have to remind her about the type of nigga I was.

"Outlaw, why you actin' like—"

"I ain't gon' tell you again. Get da fuck on."

Sucking her teeth, Briyana rolled her eyes and turned around, fanning her hand behind her as if shooing me away. I didn't say anything. I knew it was something chicks did to satisfy their hurt egos.

"You ain't gotta be so damn rude," she said, walking away. "That girl must be somethin' special."

"She is," I affirmed, knowing it would piss Briyana off but not caring either way.

Janelle was special and I wasn't afraid to let anyone know it. Dumb niggas would get with a woman they prayed at night for and then forget how bad they wanted her and how desperate they'd been to win over her heart. I'd never forget the day I begged Janelle to be mine. And, if it came to it, I'd do the same shit again.

"Bruh! You ready to come in here and meet lil' man?"

I turned around and saw Yolo standing in front of Lacey's door holding his son in his arms. Both of them were smiling at me, looking like twins. I snorted out a breath, not believing that lil' Young Yellow had a kid.

"Damn right I'm ready to meet my nephew." I hopped off the trunk and started walking their way.

"This is Jeremiah," Yolo said, bending his head to look at his son. "And Jeremiah, this is your—"

"Favorite uncle," I cut in, shaking Jeremiah's tiny hand.

Although I was happy to see him, the only thing in my mind was how much I couldn't wait to lay eyes on my daughter. I was gonna give my little girl the world.

Carmella

"*B*itch, do Cree know you here?" Bryan asked and then sucked the skin of his teeth when I gave him a look that said it all. "Aw, shit, you about to get us killed!"

"We aren't going to be here that long," I said, looking at my watch as we walked through the doors of *Trouble*. "Janelle needs to hurry up!"

After finding out that I'd been acting a damn fool for no reason, accusing Cree of hiding a child that ended up to not even be his, I'd been on my best behavior. Cree woke up to head in the morning and I let the pussy put him to sleep at night. I couldn't cook for shit, but a bitch was in the kitchen like Betty Crocker every day trying to make a miracle happen. Other than staying on top of my classes, my only other priority for the past week or so had been Cree. I wanted him to know how much I appreciated him for not being a hoe like his hoe ass brothers.

But then I remembered something that I'd wanted to follow up on but had been distracted from. That night when Cree had pulled me out of the club, Trevor… Vick—whatever the hell that nigga's name was—had said something about Cree screwing some woman over while he was locked up.

"Janelle probably knows you got us on a suicide mission and decided to skip out. Why you couldn't just ask Cree about this?" Bryan asked, pulling some huge shades on his face like he was working undercover. I just couldn't with his ass.

"I can't ask that nigga about shit right now after all the stunts I just pulled! I'm surprised he didn't strangle me for going to his grandma's house!" I cut my eyes at Bryan, watching him pull the hood on his jacket up over his head. "What the hell are you doin'?"

With wide eyes, he gawked at me like I should've already known.

"Bitch, what it look like?! If that crazy muthafucka you dating come up in here, my ass is runnin' to the nearest exit." He scoffed and rolled his eyes before pressing his fingertips to his forehead like he was stressed. "I just don't know how I keep letting you convince me to do this shit with you. He loves your ass but he don't give a damn about me, so who you think would be the one caught up? It's always the prettiest ones who die first—"

"Shhh! There he is!"

"Who Cree?!" Bryan was twisting his neck around fast, searching for Cree, while clutching the neckline of his jacket.

"No, dummy! Trevor… he's over near the bar talking."

I watched Trevor speaking to one of the men I'd recognized from the other night. He checked his watch and then glanced towards the front of the club as if he was waiting for someone to show up. He was still just as sexy as he was the first time I'd seen him, but it did nothing for me. I was on a mission and the sooner I got the information I wanted, the sooner I could leave.

"I just don't see why you feel you gotta know *everything* about your man," Bryan was saying to my side. "No one knows *everything*. Some things we just don't need to know."

Rolling my eyes, I turned around and looked behind me just in time to see Janelle walk through the club doors looking like she'd had a long day and was about to drop that baby any minute. Even still, I had to admit that she was still beautiful. Pregnancy looked good on her and gave her a glow that seemed to make her radiate.

"'Bout damn time, Jani. What took so long?"

She cut her eyes at me. "You should just be happy I'm here. This whole plan is foolish, Carm. Whatever you want to know about Cree, you should feel comfortable asking him. And if he doesn't want to tell you… well, maybe it's best that you don't know."

She placed her hands on her hips and Bryan stood by her side, the pointed expression on his face showing exactly whose side his disloyal ass was on.

Pursing my lips, I tilted my head to the side and peered at Janelle. "Of course you would say that, Ms. Goody Two Shoes."

"I just don't want you to get in any trouble—"

"You're always worried about somebody getting in some damn trouble! Stop being an old lady all the time." I knew what I was saying would strike a nerve and it did just that. Janelle's face crumpled into a slight frown and her lips pressed together to form a tight line.

"Come on, y'all. We're going to just sit at the bar like we want to have a couple drinks. Just play it cool."

Janelle obviously wanted to object to sitting at the bar but I gave her a look and she simply clenched her jaw. We walked over to the bar as cool as we could, being that one of us was nine months pregnant and another was a man with his head ducked low and huge, dark shades on, trying his hardest to blend in with the paint on the walls. I really had to find myself a new crew.

"I'll take a passion fruit margarita, please."

Sliding into the open space right next to Trevor, I knew that he'd definitely take note of my presence. He did just that, his eyes widening before narrowing into slits when they landed on me. He chuckled a little to himself and a sly grin graced his lips.

"You're back here, huh? Things not going well with ole boy?" Trevor asked, his reference to Cree opening up the door for what I wanted to ask him.

I tossed my hair a little as I turned towards him, coolly looking him up and down.

"That depends on you, I guess."

My response grabbed his full attention. Glancing at the man who he'd been talking to, he dismissed him with a few words before turning back to me. His eyes were bright and seemed to dance a little as he peered into mine.

"Depends on me? Okay, so what I gotta do to win your heart?"

Trevor was smooth, I had to admit that. He definitely was the exact type I would have gone for in the past but those days were far behind me. My heart wasn't up for grabs anymore.

"Well, first, I wanna know something. Did you use me to get to Cree? Is that why you contacted me about coming here?" I cocked my head to the side and sipped from my margarita as I waited for his answer. It was my first alcoholic drink since before going to rehab and to say that it was delicious was definitely an understatement.

"Hell no, I wouldn't do no lame shit like that." Trevor laughed. "I didn't know you was with him… and how would I know? Ain't like you got that nigga on your page. But when he came in here, seeing him fucked with me a little."

The sparkly glimmer that had been in Trevor's eyes disappeared and his pupils seemed to darken.

"Why?" I asked, eager to know what it was that Trevor and Cree had between them. Trevor's head lowered so that his gaze met mine, and it almost seemed like he'd been so into his own thoughts, he'd forgotten about me being there.

"Eight years ago, I caught a case. I could've got out after a year but I wouldn't snitch to get the reduced sentence. Cree got arrested with me but his brothers made sure he got out easy. They always say that the law can't touch the Murrays and that's the fuckin' truth. It's one of the ways Outlaw got his name… that nigga been arrested more than them all."

Well, I definitely didn't know that. In fact, I didn't even know Cree had ever been arrested at all. Cree didn't even seem like the troublemaking type. He was always so laid back and kept to himself… then again, the day he came and snatched my ass right up off the dancefloor, he was on some other shit. So maybe Trevor's story wasn't so farfetched.

"I didn't know Cree all that well. He knew my cousin and we all linked up to do stupid shit and get money. The cops told me I could do less time if I snitched, but I didn't say shit… didn't give Cree up even though I barely knew him because I wasn't raised to be no rat. Going in, I figured that it would be hard but with my girl by my side, it wouldn't be as bad as it could've been. She made sure a nigga was good, wrote me letters and shit… sent me some flicks…"

He grinned and a faraway gaze entered in his eyes as he traveled down memory lane.

"She was my world. After some time, the letters were less and less but I thought it was just because she was tryin' to get into college and was stressin', studyin' and all that. Then about a year and some change in, all that shit came to a stop. I contacted some niggas on the outside and they told me she started fuckin' with Cree and was claimin' to be his girl now. Fucked up thing was that he ain't even really want her like that. Discarded her like trash and I spent the next six years of my sentence doing hard time with nobody writing me, visiting me… none of that shit. I did my time and didn't say a word about any of them, but what did I get?"

Finished with his story, he grabbed the glass of brown liquor in front of him and downed it in one gulp. I watched him, feeling a range of emotions, none of them being what I expected I would feel after hearing Trevor out. Mainly, I was just disappointed that I'd spent the last couple of hours getting ready to come out here and listen to Trevor's punk ass! In a nutshell, Trevor was just a nigga scorned and couldn't anybody do a thing about that. He was a grown ass man who had gotten played like a sucker, and he needed to get over it.

The only part of his story that really stuck with me was how he didn't snitch for a shorter sentence. Call me selfish, a snitch, rat, or whatever else you could think of, but if it ever came down to me spending years in prison or telling on some muthafucka I didn't even know… let's just say, it wouldn't even take the normal 48 hours for them to convince me. I'd be in that bitch singing out every detail I knew right in the back of the damn cop car. They wouldn't even have to bother taking my ass to the jail!

"I'm sorry to hear all that," I told Trevor, pressing my lips together to hide my disappointment. He was such a waste of good looks because there was nothing sexy about a man who was all butt hurt and devastated over some female.

"It's all good." Standing up, Trevor sighed and then placed his hand on the bar counter, right on top of mine. "It was good seeing you… you should come around more often. Maybe we can—"

"Yeah, it was good seeing you too!" I interrupted loudly and snatched my hand away from his.

Before he could say anything else, I turned towards Bryan and gave Trevor the back of my head. If he thought I was going to help him get revenge on Cree by letting him get all in my face, it wasn't happening. Maybe in some alternate universe, a woman would cheat on somebody like Cree for Trevor, but that wasn't happening in this one.

"Can you believe that?" I asked, rolling my eyes at Bryan. "So basically I wasted my time again. Cree really is some rare man with no side hoes, no hidden baby mamas, no weird fetishes..."

Janelle leaned forward and frowned in my face. "Luke doesn't have any of those either."

I rolled my eyes to the sky and shook my head. In my opinion, the jury was still out on Outlaw's faithfulness. I liked him, but I'd never met a man that gotdamn fine who didn't have a side bitch stashed somewhere for a rainy day. Well, not until I met Cree anyways.

"I've never believed a man could be faithful. That's why I stopped taking them seriously because, as fine as I am, I've never had one not cheat!" I continued ranting. It seemed the liquor was loosening my lips.

"Oh my god!" Janelle said, much too dramatic for what I was saying but I appreciated her at least trying to make it seem like she understood what I was going through.

Amazed and still slightly shocked, I dropped my head into my hands. All of this sneaking around, being suspicious and following Cree only to find out that he was exactly the person he said he was. There was nothing to find because he wasn't lying to me.

"I know! All this time it's like I'm waiting for something bad to happen... Maybe I feel like I don't deserve to be in love and that's why I keep messing—"

"Bitch, ain't nobody worried about your selfish ass right now!" Bryan yelled, ripping my arm away from my face and shaking it hard as if were on fire. "Janelle's water just broke! We gotta get to the hospital now!"

With wide eyes, I jumped up and looked at the both of them in utter shock and surprise. Janelle was standing up with her hand on her belly and her face twisted up in pain while Bryan stood next to her, jumping up and down, squealing, and hopelessly flinging his arms in the air.

"Oh shit!" I cursed, jumping up and down. I didn't think I'd be so excited about my sister having a baby, because I really didn't do children, but now that the moment was here, I guess things changed.

"I didn't drive! I took a cab here." Janelle seemed like she was on the verge of panic.

"We can all use my car," Bryan offered, wrapping his arm around Janelle to usher out the club. "Breathe, baby! Breathe!"

"I *can't* breathe!" Janelle was almost hysterical by now, wringing her hands together in front of her. "Daddy isn't due in town for another week… the baby isn't even supposed to come for another *two* weeks! I can't have her now! She's gotta go back up there!"

Bryan snapped his neck in Janelle's direction. "Baby girl, I'm no expert on babies or vagina but I'm pretty sure you can't just suck her back up when she's trying to come out. Your daddy will be okay. We gotta get you out of here now!"

"Carmella, use my phone to call Luke!" Janelle yelled through gritted teeth, still rubbing her belly ferociously like she was trying to put out a fire. I nodded my head and grabbed her phone to do just as she asked. This was so insane… the craziest moment of my life. I couldn't believe that after everything that my sister and I had gone through together—the good things and the bad—she was about to be a mother.

"Where the hell is my car?!" Bryan shrieked, grabbing my attention from the phone. It was at that moment I realized his car wasn't at the spot we'd left it only about an hour ago.

"Oh my god! Bry, it's been towed. This is a no parking zone," I told him, pointing to a sign that we hadn't seen before. I slapped my hand to my forehead and tried to figure out what the quickest way to get to the hospital would be.

"Aye! Small ass world, ain't it, Mrs. Murray," I heard someone say. Focusing on the voice, I frowned deeply when I saw a large man, easily well over six feet, walking towards Janelle. Upon further scrutiny, I noticed that he was covered nearly head to feet in tattoos, so many covering his beefy, muscular arms that it seemed to darken his toffee-brown complexion. Behind him were a group of men who watched attentively as he walked over to where we all stood. Beside where the men stood was a line of black SUVs, Cadillacs, Expeditions, and Surburbans. What the hell was going on? Did Janelle join a gang while I was creeping around after Cree?

"Bone," Janelle greeted him breathlessly, attempting to force a smile. "Nice—nice to see you."

"You good? You look a little—"

"Aaahhh!" Janelle screamed out, doubling over and holding her belly. I put my hands to my ears, feeling so helpless that I was about to cry.

"She's about to have a baby!" Bryan yelled and pressed his hands to the side of his face, mirroring my stance. "Oh god, I'm about to have to deliver this baby for her right here in the street!"

Suddenly, I got an idea. Stepping up, I stood in front of Bone, definitely catching the way that he scoped out my body before finding my face. I ignored it. This was not the time to address that lusty look in his eyes.

"Um… Mr.—"

"Bone," he filled in for me, running his tongue over his full gold grill. Damn! I loved a nigga with golds!

"Bone," I repeated and glanced back at my sister who was being coached on breathing by Bryan. "How do you know my sister?"

"I'm a client of hers. I do business with Outlaw."

Music to my ears. "Well, is there any way that you can give us a ride to the hospital? I notice that you don't seem to be short on cars."

Bone nodded, licking his lips and then turned to the men behind him. "Notty, come over here and help Mrs. Murray and her friend to my car. Yayo, Omar, and Truth… I need y'all to roll out with me. And as for you…" he started, looking at me. "You can ride with me so we can get to know each other a little better. I mean, if that's cool with you."

I smiled and shook my head lightly while starting behind the man that had run over to escort Janelle to one of the SUVs. "I'm with someone. It's Cree, Outlaw's brother."

Bone's brows rose up on his face. "Yeah?" I nodded my head. Less than a second later, his expression transformed into full serious mode. Just that fast, he'd put a wall up and was making it clear that he was on one side and my ass was on the other.

"That's what's up. Please accept my apologies… I got much

respect for that nigga, Cree."

Nodding my head, I couldn't help but smile as Bone widened the space between us and made sure to keep his eyes facing forward the entire way to his car. When we got inside, he sat up front after making sure we were all secured in the back. I felt a sense of pride at how the simple mention of Cree's name put niggas on notice that I was off limits, especially men as powerful as Bone.

Every day I felt like I was learning more about the man I'd given my heart to, but the more I learned the more I was beginning to push my own insecurities to the side and realize that he was the one for me. Who knows? Maybe the next time we were rushing to the hospital for someone to have a baby, it would be me.

Nah… let me stop lying! It sounded good though!

Luke

"*D*amn, this some good ass weed, nigga. I'm high as a muthafucka."

My cousin, Gunplay, had come through for a nigga in the best way and blessed us all with some premium loud that had my head straight floating. At the moment, I was the most relaxed I'd ever been, sitting on the front porch of my grandma's crib, smoking it out with my brothers.

"Don't smoke too much of that shit, bruh. I had some of it last night and it had me seeing shit," Cree told me, and I almost choked laughing at his ass.

"What the hell was you seeing, fam?" Tank inquired with a devilish grin on his face.

Cree's brows shot up in the air. "You promise not to laugh?"

"Promise," me, Tank, Yolo, and Kane all said at once. Every single one of us knew damn well our asses was lying.

"I—I saw..." Cree licked his lips and scratched uneasily at his jaw before continuing. "I thought I saw a clown, my nigga. Running through the trees behind my crib."

There was about two seconds of silence before me, Tank, Kane, and Yolo all burst out laughing hard as hell. What you may not know is that Cree is terrified of clowns and this ain't the first time he's claimed to see them. The very first time Cree got high, I was the one who had rolled him his first blunt. We snuck outside on the balcony to smoke it and he swore that he saw clowns then. That nigga almost got our cover blown because of how fast he'd run back in the house, straight to our bedroom, and jumped under the covers. Our grandma woke up and burst through our door with a broomstick in her hand, threatening to beat all of our asses if we didn't go to bed.

"This must be some *really* good shit then… it got you going back to your first high." I chuckled a little and then took one more long pull before passing it over to Tank. As soon as I exhaled the smoke, I knew I'd be staying my ass right where I was for a couple hours because I already felt like I was walking on clouds.

Riiiiiing!

Riiiiiing!

"Damn, who da fuck ringin' the damn church bells this late?" I grumbled. Kane frowned, looking at me right in my face.

"Nigga, you trippin'? That's yo' damn phone!"

"Huh?"

Looking down, I grabbed my cell out of my pocket and saw that Kane wasn't lying. My phone was ringing and it was Janelle. I cleared my throat before I answered and tried to play it cool.

"What's good?"

"Outlaw—I mean, Luke! This is Carmella… Janelle's sister."

Frowning, I pulled the phone from my ear and looked at the screen. I couldn't have been tripping that hard. I could've sworn it said

Janelle was calling.

"Camel," I spoke slowly, feeling like my tongue weighed the same as ten bricks. "What's good?"

"Car-mel-la."

My head was spinning so I didn't even try to repeat after her.

"Yeah whateva, man. What's good?"

"Janelle is having the baby! Her water just broke while we were at the cl—I mean, at dinner somewhere. Anyways, Bryan was going to drive her to the—"

"Who da hell is Bryan?!"

"Shit! Sorry, Bryan is my friend and he's very, very gay—"

"VERY gay!" I heard a nigga I assumed was Bryan saying in the background.

"—and he was going to drive us to the hospital but his car was towed so now we're riding with Bone... some client of Janelle's and—"

"Yeah, I know Bone," I replied, wanting Carmella to hurry the hell on and get to the point where she told me that everything was alright and Janelle was fine.

"Okay..."

"Well, nigga?! Is Janelle good or what?"

I heard her suck her teeth and knew she was about to say some slick shit. Cree still hadn't figured out how to get a handle on his bitch.

"If she wasn't, don't you think I would have said that first?! Anyways, do you know the way to the hospital?"

"Shit!"

I didn't. Janelle had been bugging me about taking some tour with her so I would know where to go but I didn't really take her serious. What nigga wanted to tour a damn hospital? For real, I prayed every day I'd never have to walk into that shit because any time I'd been there it was never for anything good.

"Naw, send me the address!" I said, jumping up quick and grabbing my keys.

My heart was beating so fast in my chest but I didn't know if it *really* was thumping that fast or if it was the weed fucking with me. I'd been waiting for the moment when Janelle would have the baby and now that it was here, I felt nervous as hell about becoming a father.

"Everything a'ight?" Kane asked me as soon as I hung up the phone.

"Janelle 'bout to have the baby," I informed him, still searching around for something. What, I couldn't remember.

"Nigga, then what you waitin' for?"

"I'm lookin' for my damn keys!" I shouted, feeling like I was about to break a sweat even though it was somewhat cool outside.

"Bruh, ya fuckin' keys are in your gotdamn hands!" Cree told me before snatching the keys from me. "You ain't drivin' no damn where. I'll take your ass to the hospital myself. I warned you not to fuck with that weed like that."

I couldn't even say shit because he had a point. It was a clear sign that you were fucked up if you were searching as hard as I was for something you were holding in your hand.

"Good luck, bruh," Kane said, dapping me up before pulling me into a hug.

"Yeah whatever," I replied, but I was smiling so damn hard my face hurt.

"Outlaw gon' be a fuckin' daddy." Yolo walked up and gave me dap and a hug as well, cheesing hard. "Never thought I'd see the day."

"Me either, bruh," I told him honestly.

"Call us when we can come down, man," Tank told me, walking forward. He wrapped his arm around my shoulder and gave me an encouraging shake, laughing at what I could imagine was a crazy expression on my face. I couldn't believe this shit was really happening.

"Don't be nervous 'bout it, bruh," Tank said. "I been through this shit plenty of times. The chick do all the work and you just be there to listen and apologize while she cusses your ass out. Simple shit."

"I'll take yo' word for it, my nigga," I replied shaking my head. "Janelle been cussing my ass out the entire nine months so she should give a nigga a break."

Before I left, I ran in the house to tell my grandmother what was up and then Cree and I were on our way to the hospital. All I could think about was how, in a few hours or so, I'd be holding my baby girl.

Damn.

It sounded crazy to even say some shit like that. God was paying me back for giving me a girl, too. After all the chicks I'd ran through, treated like shit, and all the hearts I'd broken, now I was about to have a daughter of my own. One thing I knew for sure, if anybody tried to fuck around with mine, they would catch a hot ball to the dome on first sight.

"You sure you ready for this?" Cree cut his eyes at me, asking me the same damn question I was asking myself.

"Hell naw, but I ain't got no choice but to man up and—" I stopped talking when something caught my eye and I leaned over to get a better look out the window. "What da muthafuckin'..."

"What?" Cree asked and I shook my head.

"Nothing. Just thought I saw somethin'." I ran my hand over my face and then looked up, seeing Cree's eyes on me and a smirk on his face.

"The hell you saw, bruh? Let that shit be known."

I chuckled and shook my head incredulously, not even believing what I was about to say.

"Nigga, I could've sworn I just saw a big ass nigga in a clown suit running behind that building back there." Cree and I both started laughing. "This weed is strong as hell!"

Sidney

*M*y heart fluttered to life when I heard the door open and then close, announcing Yolo's presence. Even though I was devastated after learning that Yolo had a son, I hadn't seen him in days and I missed him like crazy. I wasn't mad at him. There was no way that I could be after hearing that some woman showed up after three years, telling him he had a son. It wasn't his fault. And, as a friend—*his* best friend—I knew that the whole situation had to be fucking with his head even more than it was mine. This was the moment that all women dealt with… the moment where you had to be stronger than the man you decided to be with.

"Hey," I said, planting a weak smile on my face when Yolo walked into the living room. I stood up from the sofa and walked over to him, knowing from the blank look in his eyes that he was trying to prepare himself for whatever mood I was in.

"Sid, I… I'm sorry for not comin' back. I stayed in Brooklyn for the past few days and—" Lifting my hand in the air, I stopped him from talking.

"I don't need an apology," I replied, shaking my head. Stepping close to him, I grabbed his hand and held it in mine. I waited a few minutes for his eyes to meet mine and, when they did, I saw they were filled with sorrow, but I wasn't sure about exactly what was going on in his mind. I needed to get him to talk to me.

"I just want to know how you've been and what's going through your mind."

His shoulders rose and fell as he sighed heavily, averting his eyes from my face once again.

"I feel like you're going to leave me. Having a son… it's all I ever wanted and, even though I never expected it to happen quite like this, I love him because he's mine. Before I even laid eyes on him, I knew that if Lacey allowed me to, I wanted to keep him and raise him myself. But I know you didn't ask for this and that's why I've been acting so crazy towards you. I'm just scared of what would come next with us. We just got together and made shit official. I couldn't ask you to be with me through this and I won't look at you differently if you don't stay."

So this was what it was all about. I'd figured that Yolo needing time to himself was because he was trying to deal with wrapping his head around having a child. I had never thought that he would think I'd leave him because of his child. It wasn't like he'd cheated on me.

But knowing that he wanted to raise his child himself was a blow I hadn't been expecting. It had never occurred to me that Yolo would make that move and I'd never considered it. And I'd never considered what it would mean to me if something like that happened. It meant that I would be living with him and his son and I'd have to share in the responsibilities of having a child.

It wasn't like I could just live with Yolo and continue on as if his son wasn't there. Even if he never asked me to help out, it would be expected of me at some level. As old as I was, I'd never even babysat a kid. I was a loner… besides my friends, I had no one. No siblings, no cousins, and no friends with kids who called me 'Aunty.' And what did I know about being a parent when I had no real relationship with my own? What the hell would I do living with a child?

"I—I just need a minute," I said, feeling an immense amount of pressure all of a sudden. It was almost like the room was closing in on me and I could barely breathe. My heart was telling me that Yolo needed me in this moment, but my mind was telling me that I was in over my head and needed to get away. With tears in my eyes, I ran over to the coffee table, grabbed my keys and then stuffed my feet into my shoes.

"You're leaving?" Yolo asked, and I swear I could feel the pain in his voice. It touched my soul but it still wasn't enough to stop me. I felt like I was falling into a black hole. I needed to leave and I had to go *now*.

"I'll be back," I promised him even though I wasn't so sure. Then I made the mistake of glancing into his face and saw the panic within his eyes. I knew I was causing him pain but I also knew it wouldn't be fair of me to agree to something I wasn't sure about simply to ease his mind. I needed the space to think.

Running out the door, I jumped in my car and pulled out of the driveway. With tears in my eyes, I drove, gripping the steering wheel for dear life. My cell phone began to ring and I knew it had to be Yolo calling to convince me to come back. I couldn't possibly speak to him at the moment.

Grabbing the phone, I was ready to ignore the call when I

saw it wasn't Yolo… it was Teema. My brows bent into a frown. Although Teema and I knew each other since we grew up in the same neighborhood, we weren't all that close. I'd figured that I was always too boyish for her so we never ran in the same circles. Out of sheer curiosity, I answered the call and waited for it to connect to the car's Bluetooth system.

"Hello?"

"Sidney?" she asked and waited for a response, like she hadn't called my phone in order to speak to me.

"I'm here," I replied, trying to put a little bit of a pep in my tone of voice. It was hard to force something I didn't feel but it wasn't like Teema knew me well enough to know the difference.

"I'm calling to let you know that Janelle is having the baby. She's at the hospital with her sister and Kane asked me to let you know in case you hadn't heard."

Although I worked with Janelle as her secretary and it made sense that I would want to know if she'd gone in labor, I knew that had nothing to do with Kane telling Teema to call me. For as long as I knew him, Kane was always the 'fixer' of the Murrays. If any of them argued with another or was having issues, Kane was the one who demanded that they talk and work things out before the next day.

Kane's insistence that they worked out their issues quickly grew after Tone's death. Losing Tone was a hit to them all, but Kane took it especially hard because he'd fought with Tone right before he was killed. But it didn't just end there. He hated for his brothers to fight each other and he hated for them to face difficult situations on their own. A true older brother, he tried to fix all of their issues if he could. And I knew that was the exact reason for this call.

"Thank you for telling me. I might go out there later," I replied back to Teema.

"Uh huh, well, where are you now?" Her question came too quickly and it affirmed my thoughts that Yolo was the main reason for Kane putting her up to this call.

"Just driving around."

"Okay, good! Can you pick me and Kenya up? Kane isn't here and I need a ride to the hospital." My lips twisted up at her words. It was a terrible lie.

"You need a ride?" I queried with suspicion. "Something wrong with all seven of them cars y'all got over there?"

There was a long pause and I knew Teema was trying to figure out a way to cover her lie.

"Shit," she said finally. "Listen, Kane told me to call and make sure you were alright after Yolo called him flipping out about you leaving and driving reckless and some other shit. Now I'm not one to be all in folk's business, but I do want to let you know that, even though we don't know each other all that well, I am here for you. As far as I'm concerned, we are family."

The second she said that, I heard Kenya yell out 'Mommy' in the background, and it totally broke me all the way down. Before I knew it, I was crying so hard that I could barely see the road, wailing and heaving out heavy breaths as if I'd been told I was living my final days. Making a sharp right, I pulled into an empty storefront parking lot and placed the car in park before throwing myself over the steering wheel.

"Um… Sidney?"

"I—I can't do this!" I began sobbing my heart out, my words bringing to life all the thoughts in my head. "I love Yolo so much—we are finally together and then *this* happens. I just want to be happy! Why does everything have to be so haaaaarrrrrdddd?!"

Yes, I'm perfectly aware that I was having the meltdown of my life while on the phone with someone who probably thought I'd lost all of my sanity, but I didn't care. Being more 'boy' than 'girl' for all of my life, I'd become used to holding things in and being tough. In this instance, I couldn't fake it anymore. I was *terrified* of committing to being with Yolo and being a mother to someone, and knowing that crushed me because I knew it meant I had to make the hardest decision of my life. I couldn't be with him anymore.

"Sidney, what is hard?" Teema asked me just as I was in the middle of blowing my nose on a piece of a napkin I found in my car. It smelled like old, greasy fries. I tossed it and reached behind my seat for the box of Kleenex I kept in my car, but when my hand came up, I was holding a shirt—*Yolo's* shirt. I started to cry even harder.

"I have to break up with Yolo. He wants to raise his son and… I can't be a mother. I'm not ready for that responsibility. I've never even been around a kid."

"Who says you have to be a mother?" Teema half-shouted through the other line. "From what I recall, Yolo's son already has a mother."

I heard Teema suck her teeth and I braced myself because, even though I had no idea why, I felt like I was about to get my ass handed to me about something.

"See, this is the same shit I went through when I was dating. Just because I had a daughter didn't mean I was looking for a nigga to be her daddy. No, her father wasn't in her life but I took care of my baby just fine on my own! Yolo became a father but that doesn't make you an instant mother just because you're in a relationship with him. The only thing he expects you to do is be respectful of his role as a father and to be respectful and kind to his son, when and *if* you meet him. Now if you marry him, that's another thing, because as his wife, he would expect you to treat his son as you would your own so that it doesn't cause issues if y'all have other children. But right now, y'all are just dating and you *just* started doing that so, girl, calm down!"

By the time Teema said her last word, I was no longer crying. It was hard to push out a tear when someone was telling you about yourself the way she was doing me.

"You're right," I admitted, realizing that I'd gone overboard without even taking a minute to listen to what Yolo was asking me. He never asked me to share in his responsibility as a father, he only wanted me not to leave him because of it.

"I know I'm right." I almost smiled at Teema's snappiness. "But I do want to know… do you ever want children? I mean, we both know how Yolo is about kids. If you don't ever want to have any, that could be an issue."

I sighed deeply and took a few seconds to think about what she was asking me. She was definitely right. I knew how Yolo felt on the issue, but how did I feel?

"I just don't wanna fail," I admitted to Teema and, for the first time, to myself what my fear was. "My mama made one mistake and it messed up the way I saw her for the rest of her life. We have no relationship at all because of that. I'm afraid of being responsible for a child and doing the wrong thing."

Never before had I admitted, either aloud or in my head, that my love for my own mother changed the day she pushed me into aborting the child I would have had with Yolo. The second I had that abortion, something about how I felt about her also died. It was something I wasn't able to come back from.

"Girl, if anyone knows about having a mama who ain't shit, it's me." A forced chuckle escaped her lips before she continued. "My mama was probably the worst there is and I never stopped loving her until it got to the point when I saw the love I had for her was starting to hurt me. Still, I know that her mistakes aren't mine. When I look at Kenya, I know that I would never do her wrong because I love my daughter more than I love myself. When you have a kid, you're always going to be afraid of doing something wrong, but the fact that you're fearful of that is proof enough that you won't. Parents who ain't worth shit aren't afraid at all because they don't give a damn."

It was like a door, that I hadn't even known was closed, opened and light came through.

"Teema, if I would've known you had all the answers, I would've started talking to you a long time ago," I said with a smile. She laughed and before I knew it, I was laughing too.

"I don't have all the answers, I can promise you that. But when you have lived the life that I've lived, you can't help but learn a few things. Now when will you be here because we are ready."

My mouth dropped open and I frowned. "Huh? Wait... you still want me to pick you up?"

"Duh!" Teema shot back, sucking her teeth. "Ain't nothing changed. I still need a ride to the hospital. I'll be on the front porch waiting for you to get here."

Before I could object, Teema hung up the phone, leaving me in the car in my thoughts. My head was much clearer than it had been previously but I knew that Yolo was probably back at the house going insane. Grabbing my phone, I went to send him a text and saw that he'd sent me one already.

Yolo: I love you, Sid. No matter what, you'll always be my one.

A warm feeling came over me, covering me completely from my head to my toes. It was a great thing to be in love but it was rare to have what I had with Yolo. He was my *first and only* love. We had a connection that was magnetic, pure, and true. No matter what happened, it was hard to lose the love you had for your first.

I love you too. You're my one, my only. See you tonight.

Yolo: Can't wait.

Feeling much lighter in spirit and state of mind, I pulled back onto the road and started towards Kane and Teema's house. Our love had been tested and, once again, we'd proven that no matter what, we were destined to be. It was complicated but, no matter what, our love would always pull through.

Janelle

Never in my wildest dreams did I think that I would be escorted to the hospital by a kingpin and his group of thugs, but here I was being carried through the halls of the maternity ward, cradled in Bone's arms with Carmella and Bryan behind me, all of us surrounded by Bone's men.

"Um… do we need all of them to walk with us?" I heard Bryan ask nervously from behind Bone. The stares we were getting from everyone around were a little unnerving, but I was struggling too hard to breathe to protest.

"You never wanna be caught slippin," Carmella replied as if she was the expert on the thug life. If I wasn't trying to get through another excruciatingly agonizing contraction, I would have rolled my eyes.

"Uggghhhh!"

"We're almost there," Bone assured me. "I just had my seventh son so I know exactly where to go."

"Seventh?!" I asked once the contraction subsided.

Smiling, Bone looked down at me and nodded his head. "And all from the same woman, too. We ain't together anymore but I take care of her because she takes good care of mine."

My mouth nearly fell to the floor, and it probably would have if another contraction hadn't followed so quickly behind his statement.

I was in so much pain right now that I knew damn well there was no way I would ever be having another child. It didn't matter what Luke said or how much he pleaded with me, I'd get a surrogate before we did this again.

We arrived at the check in counter and I was hit with a contraction so intense that I felt myself go faint in Bone's arms, and knew I was losing consciousness when I started to see dark spots. I felt like the walls of my vagina were being ripped apart.

"We gotta get her to a room, now!" I heard a woman yell out and I began to feel weaker. Another contraction came and I winced.

"Janelle? What's wrong with her?"

Luke.

My eyes fluttered at the sound of his voice as I struggled to stay awake. I felt so tired.

"I got her," I heard him say, and Bone handed me over with ease.

Sweat covered my forehead and I still felt weak, but knowing that I was in Luke's arms relaxed me. Feeling him kiss me lightly across my forehead as he carried me to the room, I suffered through my contractions a little easier than before.

"The doctor will be on his way to introduce himself," a nurse said after making sure I was comfortable inside of the room I'd been given. "Do you need anything before I go?"

She performed a series of exams, stuck her hand all up in my private areas, and was satisfied that there was nothing out of the ordinary happening. I felt much better, having had my epidural and no longer experiencing such excruciating pain. Looking at the nurse, I shook my head and watched as Bone and Luke smacked hands in greeting.

"I can't thank you enough for bein' there when I needed you, fam," Luke was saying with a grin on his face. "I owe you big time, man."

Bone shook his head. "You can never owe me shit, Outlaw. It's all good. And congratulations, nigga!" Luke's grin grew even wider. "Aye, send me a pic when the princess comes into the world."

"I'll do just that. Stay on the lookout for a wedding invitation, too. We were supposed to get the shit done before the baby, but I guess the lil' one ain't wanna wait."

A stabbing feeling passed through my chest when I thought about that. I was disappointed about not being married before giving my birth to my daughter. Although everything else about my life had not gone according to plan, I really wanted at least this one thing.

"Word? Well, nigga, you know Preach can do it. He do it for everybody."

Luke turned to look at me, his brows high in the air and his eyes wide. Cree, Carmella, and Bryan, all sitting on a small sofa in the corner of the room, were staring at me in the exact same way. Everyone was waiting to see what I'd say.

"Uh... I guess?"

Bone lifted his hand and snapped his fingers, alerting one of his crew that was standing outside of the door.

"Aye, tell Preach to come in here."

With a goofy smile on his face, Luke walked over and stood by my side. Even though I was in a near state of shock about what was happening, I managed to put a smile on my face.

"Y'all already got the marriage license?" Preach asked after Bone filled him in on what he was being asked to do. He looked youngish, with a very clean-cut style, large, soft eyes and designer glasses on his face. Even though he wore street clothes, the collar of his shirt had a white band going through it, like the kind priests wore, and hanging off his neck was a long, gold chain with a cross at the end.

I nodded my head. "Yes… we got it a while ago, I've just been holding on to it. It's at the house."

Preach seemed to be relieved at that. "Then we can get it done. I'll sign the paperwork later but that's just a formality. As far as God is concerned, once we are finished, you'll be man and wife."

Luke ran his hand over his head, like he couldn't believe what he was about to do, and I gave his hand a squeeze.

And then right there, under God, I—Janelle Pickney—became Janelle Murray, thanks to a drug dealer who doubled as a preacher, with his kingpin boss, Carmella, Cree, and Bryan as my witnesses.

I couldn't believe my life. This wasn't according to plan! But I guess it was like they said: We make plans and God laughs.

"Okay, it's time to deliver this baby," the doctor said and my heart thrummed with anticipation.

It was about an hour after I'd become Mrs. Murray and, even though I was so exhausted, it was time to get to business. I looked to my left and felt a sense of happiness and joy I'd never felt before when

I looked at Luke and saw the love in his eyes. He lifted my hand and brought it to his lips, kissing it softly.

"You got this, Nell. Bring our baby into the world."

Gritting my teeth, I mustered up all the focus I could and pushed everything from my mind except what Luke had asked me to do. Of all the things I'd studied hard to excel in, I knew that this was the most important thing I'd ever do and I hadn't studied a single day to prepare for it. But that was okay, because with my husband by my side, I knew I could give birth to our child.

And I did just that.

About 45 minutes after my first push, January Lukeisha Murray, came into the world, screaming to the top of her lungs. I cried tears of joy the second I heard her little voice, and I know I saw Luke wipe at his eyes even though he swore later on that he definitely did not shed any tears. January's eyes stayed closed until the moment they laid her in my arms and she heard her father's voice. Her tiny eyes opened wide and she looked at both of us before her lips pulled up into the cutest little smile.

No, this wasn't the way I'd wanted my first child to come into the world. I'd imagined that I would check myself into the hospital at exactly 40 weeks to deliver my baby with my hair freshly done, nails manicured and pedicured and my husband with the video recorder on deck. I'd imagined that I would have exactly an hour or two of preparation before the doctor came inside and told me that it was time to push. And when it was time, I'd always imagined I'd have my husband and mother in the room, with my father and sisters waiting for the good news out in the hall.

In the end, I didn't get a single thing that I'd imagined. But my baby girl was absolutely perfect. In the end, that was all that really mattered.

Carmella

"$\mathcal{K}$inda makes you think about havin' one, huh?" Cree asked me while staring down at January as she slept in the newborn nursery.

Hands down, she was the cutest baby I'd ever seen. So tiny, so fragile, but still so strong. Even though she was only a few hours old, you could tell she would be just as stubborn as both of her parents. It was unimaginable how she'd just come into the world and I loved her so much already… enough to know I'd give my life for her. And she was only my niece! I would be a million times worse with my own child. And everybody knew I was the most selfish person in the world, so that was saying a lot.

"She does make me think of that," I replied honestly to Cree, not taking my eyes off January's peaceful face. "She's so beautiful… it's incredible to think of how she just came into the world. She wasn't here only hours ago, and now she is. She changed Janelle and Luke's whole life that quickly. She's changed my whole life."

When I didn't hear Cree respond right away, I looked at him and saw that his eyes were on me, staring at me with an expression that I can't explain, but that I felt so strongly. It was more than a regular love. The look in his eyes was one of pure satisfaction, comfort, and admiration. He seemed to be at peace with me. I felt the same exact way about him.

"You ever think about what it would mean if you were my wife?" he asked, sending me into a near state of shock. I recovered quickly and immediately shot back my own flippant response, something I did as a way of protecting myself when I felt like he was pulling out feelings that I wanted to keep hidden inside.

"Why does that sound like you trying to own me? How about do you ever think about what it would mean to be my husband?" I cocked my head to the side with a smirk.

Cree ran his hand over the top of his head and shook it slightly, like he couldn't believe what he was thinking.

"I ain't never thought I'd be anyone's husband. Shit... never thought I'd be anyone's man. But I do know that I wanna make you mine when the time is right." He licked his lips and I swear it made my whole body quiver. "I know you like bein' your own person—you're like me that way because I damn sure love bein' my own man. But when I cool down with this shit I'm doin' and I'm just a dentist... I want you to be there with me."

That was something I'd never promised any man—mainly because I never thought a man worthy enough for me to stick around for, not even for more than a couple weeks. Sure, I'd been in relationships before but none of them were all that serious because I never felt comfortable enough to get my feelings involved.

"I'll be there with you," I told him with pure honesty.

A goofy smile rose up on Cree's face. "Good."

He grabbed my hand and turned to walk away but then I

remembered something. I needed the same reassurance from him.

"Wait! What about me?" I started and he frowned deeply, crinkling his brows up on his forehead. "What about sticking with me? It's no secret that you don't agree with the things that I do with my life. I like attention, I like showing my body… I like partying. Will you stick with me through all of that and believe in what I do even if you don't like it?"

It was a loaded question and I knew it. I wasn't just asking Cree to be with me while I made a name for myself, I was asking for him to be comfortable with sharing me with my fans, allowing men to lust after me and say things that would normally get their asses kicked, but just let it fly. It was hard to explain to him that I did this not just because I got a high from it… but I was good at it! I wasn't even trying to get paid to party, I was just having fun with Bryan and BAM—it became a paid opportunity for me.

"If that's what you wanna do, I'm good with it. But shit is gonna be different from now on… I don't feel comfortable with you goin' out there and partyin' with drunk ass niggas and Bryan's your only protection." Cree didn't wait for a response or explain himself further but I didn't need to hear anything else. I was just happy to know that I had his support along with his love.

"Great, because I got a few things lined up tonight. I took some time off but it's time to get back on it. Mama's gotta make some money!" I smiled brightly and added a little extra bounce in my step as we stepped on the elevators.

"*We* got a few things lined up," Cree said and I pushed my lips to the side, not really knowing what he was talking about. I didn't ask either and I definitely regretted that later.

God, *why* didn't I ask?

***

"Um… Carm, should I remind you that you get paid to actually look like you're having fun?" Bryan poked me in my side as we sat at the bar. "You look more like you're at a funeral instead of the hottest spot in the city right now."

Groaning, I dropped my chin into my palm and pouted while leaning on the bar countertop. Yes, the spot was live and the club was packed damn near to capacity. The DJ was playing all the hits and, normally, I would've been having the time of my life… except there was one problem.

"How the hell am I supposed to dance and have a good time with Cree's eagle eyes on me?"

I glanced up to the second floor where V.I.P. was and frowned at Cree who was sipping from a red cup and staring right at me. Seeing that I was looking at him, he lifted his hand and waved, wiggling his fingers slightly and tossing me a teasing grin. He knew he was fuckin' up my vibe. Next to him was his brother, Yolo, who seemed to be having a good time… a much better time than I was having.

"Why don't you just have a drink to loosen up a little?" Bryan asked, signaling to the bartender. "You never drink usually because Cree isn't around. But he's here so take a few shots to let loose and let's get the party started. I wore my good jacket tonight and I'm ready to get up under them lights and show out!"

Twisting around on his chair, Bryan held up his silver sequined jacket and struck a few poses with his lips poked out that made me laugh. He was fly to the max, wearing a black fedora hat with a silver feather sticking out the top, black skinny jeans and silver sequined platforms that matched the jacket. I matched his fly in a short, gold sequined dress, paired with some heels that made my legs look better than Serena Williams' but I had yet to even try to show them.

"Here, take this." Bryan pushed three shot-glasses in my face and I eyed them suspiciously, the way that Janelle used to do when I made her drink my mystery drinks.

Shit... was I acting like Janelle?

Thinking over that was all I needed to make me grab the glasses and down each one quickly, one behind the other. The last thing I wanted was to be mentally comparing myself to my stick-in-the-mud older sister! I was Carmella Pickney, the one who got paid to get the party started and there was no way that Cree should be able to stop that!

"Damn, that burned going down. What the hell was in that?" I grimaced and smacked my lips, trying to rid the taste of the liquid from my tastebuds.

"Don't worry about that. Just get your ass up and let's get this party started!"

Bryan grabbed my hands and I, reluctantly, allowed him to pull me onto the dancefloor. Once we got there, he started framing his face, doing some 'vogue' move that had me about to pass out from laughing so hard. I mimicked his moves as we laughed and cut up on the dancefloor. Bryan was definitely my hype man.

In such a short time, he'd become my best friend. After what her brother put me through, I hadn't spoken much to Sasha anymore. I knew it wasn't her fault that I'd gotten wrapped up in all the bullshit but, once everything started going down and I was getting publicly shunned because of the promotions, I'd noticed that she'd started calling me less and less. Not just that, I'd realized that Sasha and I had become friends based on the fact that we both were women scorned, women so used to men using us that we used our bitterness to get along. Once things started going well between Cree and I, she didn't seem to be happy for me at all. But with Bryan around, I didn't miss her one bit.

"Pop that lil' booty, girl!" Bryan egged me on as I danced hard as hell to a new Cardi B song like I was trying to audition to be one of her backup dancers. Cree was absolutely the last thing on my mind.

I saw a woman grab Bryan's arm and whisper something in his ear but I just kept dancing, not missing a beat or a single photo op from the people who were watching me tear it up on the dancefloor. A few people in the club knew who I was and the ones who didn't just stared curiously, trying to figure out who the girl was that everyone was in awe about.

"Bitch, she told me that Rihanna just commented on your page and followed you! She said she's headed here because you said it's the spot to be. Heffa, we made it!"

With my mouth wide open, I turned around to look at Bryan who was jumping up and down and I joined right in, screaming nearly to the top of my lungs. I loved Rihanna more than I loved my damn self. She was my sister in my mind and I would give my right arm for the chance to meet her.

"I'm about to fuckin' diiiiiiiieee!" I screamed out, fanning myself like I was going to pass out.

"Girl, you better die *after* you get some pics with her. Let's hit the bathroom right now. I gotta freshen up your make up. I can't believe I'm almost famooooouuuuus!" Bryan flapped his arms and hands in the air as he ran around in a circle, celebrating to himself before collecting himself enough to grab my arm and drag me to the bathroom.

Making good on her Instagram comment, the Navy queen herself showed up and graced us all with her presence, for a short time but still long enough for me to almost lose my entire mind. It was so surreal meeting her that I almost cried real tears. But what blew my mind is that she didn't even act like a celebrity. She was cool as hell, like hanging out with a normal person instead of someone as accomplished as she was.

"Where's Cree?" she'd asked right before she was about to leave. "He told me he was goin' to be here. I need to get up with my homeboy before I leave."

"*Cree?!*" I shrieked, not fully believing that I'd heard what she was saying. "Cree is your homeboy?"

She smiled at my question. "Yeah, he told me about your gig tonight and asked me to swing by before I left town."

There was so much about that man that I didn't know.

The next morning, I was still reeling over the fact that I'd actually met the one woman I'd thought I'd only see in my dreams. Waking up with a smile on my face, I rolled over to give Cree some premium head, my way of thanking him for making so many of my dreams come true.

"Daaaammmn, that's how you treatin' a nigga now?" he moaned, placing his hand behind my head as I deep-throated him like a pro. "Don't you think you thanked me enough last night?"

With my mouth full, I couldn't answer but I didn't need to because I was sure he got it. I slurped and spit on his dick, rolling it around in my mouth before speeding up my pace, just about swallowing him whole, not even gagging. Never one to be able to get head without getting a sample of the pleasure I held between my legs, Cree reached down and grabbed me up under my arms, lifting me up before lowering me right on top of his erection. I gasped as he impaled me so sweetly that I nearly came on the spot.

Rolling my hips around on him, I enjoyed the way that my pussy made a smacking sound. I had that gushy shit and I could tell by the way that Cree was rocking up even more inside of me that it was driving him crazy. My phone started ringing but we both ignored it, our senses so concentrated on each other that nothing else mattered. I rode him like I was an award-winning jockey, jumping up and down on his dick like it was giving me life. He grabbed me up just at the exact moment that I was about to make him cum and flipped me around, slamming me face-first onto the bed. With my legs closed, he entered me from behind, stroking me hard while squeezing his hand around my neck. He sped up the pace and pushed my head even further down into the bed, to the point that I couldn't breathe, fucking me hard like it was the last time he'd ever get to experience pussy this good. He came hard, gritting his teeth as his dick contracted within my walls and then pulled it out at the very last minute and sprinkled his seed on my ass.

He released my head and I was only able to take a single gulp of air before he flipped me around and dove between my legs, sucking on my clit like a vicious animal. I screamed out nonsense and hollered to the heavens as he sucked and licked on me, vacuuming up my juices while moaning out his testimony of how good it was to him. Arching my back, I tore at the sheets with my hands and shrieked as I came hard, releasing my sweet elixir as he lapped it up hungrily.

Cree was in the shower and I was about to join him when I suddenly remembered that someone had been blowing up my phone. I grabbed it and frowned slightly when I saw that I had about a dozen or more texts from Bryan and five calls.

Bitch! You made it to TMZ, The Shaderoom and Entertainment Tonight!

I clicked on the many links Bryan had sent and quickly read the headline of each story. By the time I got to the last one, I was jumping up and down, hooting and hollering like I was in somebody's church and had just caught the Holy Ghost.

Who is This Girl? Beautiful Mystery Woman Steals the Spotlight from Rihanna! read the headline for Entertainment Tonight.

Under the headline was a photo of me and Rihanna that she'd posted on her Instagram page. While she looked as beautiful as ever, standing in a simple pose with her hand up and fingers forming the peace sign, I'd put my all in the picture and was stunting on them in a side pose that showed my ass, all my curves, my large breasts and was giving my best flirty, sexy expression. The comments under each article spoke about how gorgeous I was and a few people who had heard about me shared stories about how it was partying with me. Then I checked my Instagram page and nearly passed the hell out when I saw that I'd ballooned up to over a million followers. This was crazy!

"Mel? You comin'?" Cree asked, sticking his head out of the bathroom door.

"Cree, Rihanna posted our picture on her page and made me famous!"

With my tongue out, I dropped down and started doing a naked twerk. Snickering to himself, Cree shook his head.

"I don't get what the allure is about being famous and havin' people all up in your shit but if it makes you happy..." He shrugged while I started doing the Milly Rock. Nothing could steal my joy.

"How do you know her anyways?" I asked Cree after I'd finished dancing it out. "She called you her 'homeboy'. Why didn't you tell me you knew Rihanna?"

Cree's brows furrowed. "I know a lot of people. From makin' beats."

Now it was my turn to furrow my brows. "Beats?"

Nodding his head, Cree pointed down at his computer that was sitting on the nightstand. "I keep them on there if you wanna listen to a few. While you're in class, if I'm not working on something, I'm in the studio... I go just about everyday."

My mouth dropped open and my eyes bugged. "Is *that* why you're always carrying that damn computer everywhere you go?" He nodded nonchalantly. "Why didn't you tell me you were making music?"

"You never asked."

Shaking my head, I couldn't help but laugh to myself about everything that was happening in my life. I'd been driving myself crazy the past couple months, determined to find out what secrets Cree had, forcing myself to believe that he was playing games on me and the truth couldn't be farther from what I'd been trying to make it. And now I was hearing that instead of all the sneaking around and snooping, all I had to do was ask.

"Let's take a shower and then you can play some for me," I told him and Cree simply nodded, like it wasn't a big deal.

Every day was a learning process for me when it came to this man. We were so different. I was so complex and he was so simple. I was full of drama and he was so low-key. I loved attention and he loved to live in the shadows. In so many ways, he was the exact opposite of me but I was determined to make it work with him because I knew, without a single doubt in my mind, that Cree was the one for me.

Sidney

"*Y*ou ready?" Teema asked me and I nodded my head, so caught up in my thoughts that I'd momentarily forgotten that I was on the phone and she couldn't see me.

"Yes," I replied, clearing my throat. "I'm ready."

"Good because he just left here so he's on the way home."

After watching Janelle holding January in her arms, I found myself pining for something that I never thought I'd ever want for myself. But seeing the love in her eyes that she had for her daughter brought tears to mine. It was so beautiful being a witness to the kind of love that a mother had for her child and I was certain that one day I wanted it for myself.

That night, I sat down with Yolo and we had a long talk about our relationship and the changes that would come about in his life now that he had a son. Just as he'd wanted, Lacey agreed to let Jeremiah live with him, saying that it was good for him to have his real father in his life. Today, Yolo was bringing Jeremiah home for the first time and I had asked Yolo if I could be there to meet him.

"I'm actually kinda excited about it," I admitted to Teema, surprising even myself when I thought about it. "I can't wait to see Yolo's interaction with his son. We finished his room yesterday and Yolo was so happy the entire time we were getting it together."

Smiling, I thought back to the night before when we were putting the finishing touches on Jeremiah's room. Yolo was the type of person who was just naturally good at everything he put his mind to so I didn't know why I was so surprised to see that he had an artistic side. He painted the most beautiful mural on Jeremiah's wall of a lion, elephant and zebra, taking his time because he wanted it to be perfect. His room looked like a toddler's heaven, complete with a basketball goal, any toy that he could imagine and clothes so stylish that Jeremiah would look like he was ready for a runway each day. Yolo went all out for his kid.

"We will be coming over there later on this week to visit and see what y'all did with the room." Teema paused and then sucked her teeth. "On second thought, maybe not. Kane has been at my ass about trying for another baby because he wants a son so I better not let him see Jeremiah's room. I might have to kill his ass afterwards."

Giggling, I rolled my eyes. I already knew that battle with Kane was one that Teema would lose. He'd made it known that after bringing Kenya into his life, he had no intentions of slowing down when it came to having kids. Kane had already started putting more attention into growing his legitimate businesses so that he could fall into the family life and leave the streets behind him.

I heard the sound of a car approaching and jumped up from the sofa to check outside. My stomach started churning when I saw Yolo's car pulling up into its normal position.

"They are here!"

"Okay, just take a deep breath and relax, okay?"

My mouth seemed to go dry. "W—what if he doesn't like me?"

Teema sucked her teeth and I knew that she was rolling her eyes even though I couldn't see her. "Girl, he is a child! He likes everybody!"

I hung up the phone with Teema and started wringing my hands together, my eyes dancing around the house, inspecting it to make sure everything was perfect.

Chill, Sidney. He is just a child. He won't care if the house is clean or not.

No idea why I was trippin' but I definitely was. You would think I was about to meet Barack and Michelle Obama. Even though I'd seen Jeremiah before when he was at Grandma Murray's house, I was so shocked after hearing the news that I could barely remember what he looked like and I definitely hadn't spent any real time with him. Now I was nearly about to panic. My nerves were on edge.

The door opened and I sucked in a breath, holding it in as I waited.

"We're here!" Yolo announced, walking in. In his arms was Jeremiah, looking just as cute as ever. I watched as his little eyes scoped the room, taking in his new surroundings before they finally landed on me.

"Sidney!" he screamed and began reaching out for me to hold him. Laughing, Yolo placed him down and he immediately ran over to me, wrapping his tiny arms around my legs and squeezing tight.

Shocked beyond words, I looked up at Yolo with my lips parted and my eyes wide, silently questioning him.

"Don't look at me like that," Yolo replied with his hands up in surrender. "I don't know why he's acting like that. All I told him was your name."

Looking down at Jeremiah as he hugged me tight in his tiny arms, I felt a change inside of me. Once he let go, I bent down and looked right into his eyes, seeing so much of Yolo within them. I fell in love with him instantly.

"I made cookies… you want some?" I asked with a wide smile on my face.

"I wove cookies!" He started to jump up and down, his excitement making me laugh.

"Okay, well, do you 'wove' them with milk?"

The jumping continued. "I wove milk!"

Without delay, I scooped Jeremiah up into my arms and took him to the kitchen, sitting him up on the countertop as I fixed his milk and cookies. As soon as I pushed them towards him, he dropped two of the cookies into the cup of milk and then grabbed the spoon. With a slight frown, I watched as he chopped the cookies with his spoon and mixed it with the milk.

"What are you doing?" I peeked into the cup, watching him while he continued chopping. With one brow lifted, he spied at me like he was trying to figure out if I could be trusted enough to know.

"It's my secret recipe. I'm makin' a magic potion," he whispered and then turned slightly, peering at me from over his shoulder like he was hiding something.

With wide eyes, I gawked at him. It was like looking at a little Yolo. When he was a child, he used to do the same thing, pulling up random herbs, mushrooms and shrubs from his grandmother's yard and mixing them together to make his 'medicine'. More than a few times, he'd made a few concoctions that he tricked me into tasting. It was a wonder I'd made it pass thirteen years old, fooling up with him.

"It's crazy, isn't it?" Yolo walked up from behind me and stood by my side, his eyes planted on his son. "I wasn't even with him for his first years but it's almost like I was."

"Taste it!" Jeremiah demanded, pushing the small cup up under my nose. His brows were knotted up on his forehead, tightly, like he expected total obedience and nothing less.

Yolo looked on with pride in his eyes as I lifted the cup and pretended to take a sip.

"Yummy! That's good," I dramatized, licking my lips and all. Jeremiah smiled and nodded like he already knew I would love it before I'd confirmed it. He was definitely his father's child. There was no doubt about that.

Later on that night, I was lying in the bed with Yolo, talking about how much fun I'd had with Jeremiah and all the things I wanted to do with him the next day when he started kissing my shoulder and fingering the waistline of my night shorts.

"What are you doin'?!" I frowned, snatching my shoulder away from his lips. "We can't do anything nasty. The baby is sleeping in there!"

"Right," Yolo mumbled, pushing his face into my neck to pepper more kisses against my skin. "He's sleepin' which means he ain't worried about shit we got goin' on in here."

"Shhhh! I think I heard him!" I nudged Yolo away and sat straight up in the bed, not making any movement so that I could hear.

"You ain't hear shit, Sid. Now lay back for a minute."

Even though I did as Yolo asked, my ears were homed in for even the smallest sound coming from Jeremiah's room. I knew that it was his first night in his new room and I wanted to make sure that he didn't get scared. But then the sudden connection of Yolo's tongue against the soft folds between my legs, took my breath away and pushed away all of my thoughts.

"Ahhh," I moaned and arched my back to push myself into him, enjoying the way he was making love to me with his mouth.

"I love you, Sid," he whispered in my ear, much later, after he'd nearly brought me to a climax with his expert tongue. With my eyes closed, I repeated the words back to him, feeling something similar to how it was to be drunk.

"I love you... shit!"

Yolo pushed into me with one sharp motion, diving straight down into me before I'd even gotten the chance to prepare for it. He had me clutching his back, trying to decide whether I wanted to take it or run away. In the end, I decided that only an idiot would run from good dick so I simply opened my hips wide and took him in.

"Say it to me again," he commanded me through gritted teeth and pushed deeper inside of me, fucking me hard. When I didn't do as he asked as fast as he wanted it, he bent down and clamped one of my nipples between his teeth, biting down just enough to make me scream.

"I love you!" I yelped, feeling a divine mixture of pain and sheer pleasure.

"Say it to me again! I didn't tell you to stop!" he said, his teeth still biting down on my nipple. He bit down a little harder and I felt my pussy pop.

"IloveyouIloveyouIloveyouIloveyouI—oh fuck!"

By the time Yolo collapsed on top of me, both of us breathing heavily as we tried to collect ourselves, my entire body was sore.

"How long I gotta wait before you give me some babies?"

My eyes shot open, thinking that I'd heard him wrong. "Huh?"

"You heard me right, Sid." He chuckled a little and then pulled up to look me in my eyes. "How long? Years? Months? Days?" Smiling, he looked down at me and waited for my answer.

"Days?" I repeated, giggling at the thought.

"I would prefer days but it's really on you." His remark threw me for one and I stopped with the giggles immediately and stared at him, wondering if he was serious. The look he gave me told me that he was.

"You already know I'm not trying to have nobody's babies without a full commitment. I don't play that shit," I half-joked with him. "Y'all niggas love to get a bitch pregnant but when it comes to actually giving her your last name, it's muthafuckin' crickets—"

Pushing something in front of my face, Yolo stopped me before I could even finish my thought, shutting me up instantly.

"Yeah you thought a nigga was on some bullshit, huh?" he asked with a smirk, knowing full well that he'd just done some boss shit that

I hadn't been expecting.

Looking at the small, black box that he was holding in his hands, I couldn't even respond. My vision blurred when tears came to my eyes and, before I knew it, I was full on crying like a big ass, emotional baby. Thinking that something was wrong with me, Yolo snatched the box away and started to panic.

"Damn, Sid! My bad if I'm movin' too fast… I just thought—I mean, we've known each other our whole lives and I've loved you since we were kids. I'm sorry, I—"

Sniffling, I shook my head at him. "No, I'm happy. I'm so fuckin' happy."

His expression changed immediately and Yolo's face lit up like he'd swallowed a million-watt lightbulb. Using just his thumb, he pushed the box open and revealed a ring that was so different from anything any woman would have expected but to me, it meant everything. I wasn't the traditional woman so Yolo didn't give me the traditional ring. Instead of a diamond, the center of the ring was a platinum basketball, covered in diamonds. On the band was our initials, 'J & S', 'J' for Jace, Yolo's government name, and a date.

"Will you marry me?" he asked, grinning so wide that his lips nearly met the edges of his eyes. I gawked back at him incredulously, knowing damn well that he knew me well enough to be able to guess exactly what I was going to say.

"Um, DUH!" I replied loudly and pushed my finger in his face. He placed the ring on my finger and I squinted at it, appreciating every detail because I knew that it was custom-made. Yolo had put his heart into this one.

"What day is this?" I asked him, pointing at the date on the band.

Yolo pretended to be shocked, his mouth falling open and his brows shooting up for the sky. "I can't believe you don't know!" I rolled my eyes at him and waited for him to explain further. "Remember the first day we met, you tossed the basketball at me, smacking me on the side of the head in front of all my brothers?"

Thinking back down memory lane, I laughed hard. I started crushing on Yolo the second I saw him but, being awkward and nervous about how to talk to a boy that I liked, I didn't know how to act when it came to him. So I went with what I knew and played it tough.

My plan had almost backfired on me. After hitting him with the ball, Outlaw and Tank fell all out on the ground laughing at him, clowning him about how the ball had knocked the hat off his head. He had been so embarrassed about being hit and got so angry that I had instantly wondered if I'd made the wrong move.

"Yeah, you told me that girls couldn't play basketball as good as boys and pissed me off. I challenged you to our first game that day and beat your ass."

Yolo screwed up his face, letting me know that he still felt some kind of way about losing to me. After winning, I rubbed it in every day, every single time I saw him until he challenged me to a rematch and beat me so bad that I ran home crying. Always the sensitive one, Yolo had showed up to my house later on that night and apologized, inviting me over to hang with him and his brothers on his grandma's porch. The entire night, Outlaw and Tank had teased him about being

195

soft and apologizing to a girl but Yolo's actions had won over my heart.

"I let you win that game," Yolo replied and I rolled my eyes, not believing it one bit. "When I think back to that day, I feel like that's when everything with us started. I had to get you this ring because, as crazy as it is, our love for basketball has always been what's held us together."

He was right. After that day, basketball was how we settled all arguments, even our secret late night rendezvous happened on the courts. It was a central part of our relationship, whether we meant for it to be or not. But, through it all, Yolo had always been my first love and basketball came second. In high school, when I was offered a scholarship to play for a college out of state, I'd turned it down to go to a school that was closer to him. Everyone called me stupid but I knew that I'd have been miserable without him.

"How long have you been holding this ring?"

Snickering, Yolo bit down on his bottom lip briefly and then shook his head. "You wouldn't believe me if I told you."

"Try me," I pressed.

With a sigh, Yolo sat up in the bed, letting the covers fall to his waist, exposing his muscular upper body.

"I bought this after we hit our first major lick."

I screwed up my face, wrinkling my nose up as I thought about when that had been. "But that was years ago... before we even went to college!"

He nodded his head, looking down at the ring on my finger

before lifting his eyes to me.

"I guess I knew all the way back then that I wanted you to be my wife. I just needed to wait for the right moment. I did a lot of stupid shit in the process... but I always knew where my heart was."

He leaned over and kissed me softly against my lips, erupting inside of me a million emotions that I couldn't quite explain but I knew that I never wanted this feeling to end. I only wished that Faviola could be here so that I could share my happiness with her. Of all people in the world, she would have been the one to understand just how amazing this moment was.

I'd loved Yolo my whole life and it definitely hadn't been easy. Many times, I second-guessed myself, felt stupid for loving him, insecure and even felt that I wasn't enough but, in the end, it became clear that from the beginning and whether he knew it then or not, I was everything he wanted. I was the happiest woman in the world and there was no way that was going to change. I loved my man and I loved my life.

Thank you for letting me share my tale of true love with you.

Luke

*W*rinkling my brows, I narrowed my eyes and clenched my jaw, determined not to lose the battle that I had just entered into. Outlaw wasn't one to lose a fight, never had and never would. Wasn't a damn thing in me that said 'loser'. No matter what it was, I came out on top. But as I stared into eyes that looked just like mine, I wondered if I'd just met my match.

"Luke! How long is it going to take you to change her diaper? You've been in there forever!" Janelle crowed from the next room but I ignored her, keeping my attention on January.

"You dropped a load in there, didn't you?"

My baby girl only smiled in response but I knew better. Behind that sweet and beautiful, God-given grin lurked a cunning warrior that used her stank ass diaper as her primary weapon. The very first time she'd put me to this kind of test, I'd failed miserably and ran out the door yelling for Janelle to take over after I'd accidentally gotten a piece of baby shit on my thumb. This time I was ready.

"I know you dropped a load because I smell it. Yo' lil' pretty ass smell like a grown man." Her smile only seemed to grow but I was dead serious. "But daddy is ready for you this time. Ain't gon' be no runnin' because I'm about to man up."

Reaching to my side for my materials, I grabbed up the latex gloves and put one on and then was pulling on the other when I heard Janelle stomp into the room.

"Hurry up, we are late for her doctor appoint—Luke! Why do you have gloves on to change my baby?" Janelle asked and then walked over and looked at the other tools I had laid out next to the changing table, lifting one of them up. "And what you need a pair of tongs for? You're changing a baby, not cooking barbecue. What is wrong with you?!"

"Man, you know what happened the last time she took a dump and I had to change the diaper. This time I came fully prepared!"

Without saying a word, Janelle just stood there giving me a blank stare before she broke down laughing so hard that she was holding her stomach and wiping tears from her eyes. I didn't see a damn thing as funny.

"Luke, you do *not* need all that to change a baby!"

Cutting my eyes at her, I curled up my lip and frowned. "You weren't the one runnin' around here with a green ass thumb after changing her diaper before!" My eyes narrowed as I looked from Janelle to January and then back to Janelle. "You know what? I think y'all in this together. How come every time you ask me to change her diaper she done shitted in it?"

Janelle didn't answer but when I saw the edge of her lips crack into a smile, I knew I'd been played.

"Oh, y'all muthafuckas think y'all smart, huh?" Reaching out, I playfully pinched Janelle's nose between the side of my index finger and my thumb. "And so the bullshit starts. I've been outnumbered by females and y'all already with the shits. Literally."

Jokes aside, I was at the best point in my life that I'd ever been in. Janelle made me the happiest man on Earth on the day that she made me a husband and a father. Imagine me doing the family thing... I couldn't see it before it happened but I damn sure loved it. It came easy to me and I knew it was shock to everyone because it was definitely a shock to me.

But even though it looked like I was following in Kane's footsteps, this was where I had to draw the line. Whereas Kane was trying to bow out the game and become a family man, that was the last thing on my mind. The streets were where I belonged and I intended on letting it stay that way. I'd find a way to balance out my home life and role as a husband and father with my street life and role as a goon but I couldn't go straight. I had a lot more gangsta shit to do.

"What's up, bruh?"

Phone to my ear, I leaned back in my leather recliner and took a long pull on the smoldering blunt between my fingers. The day we brought January home, she damn near woke up the entire neighborhood from how hard she was screaming in the middle of the night. I knew right then that it was time for me to get my man cave together. I loved my lil' girl more than life itself but her small ass had lungs strong enough to blow out glass windows. The first time she started up in the middle of the night, I jumped straight up out the bed and started searching for my strap because I thought we were under attack.

"We still got that job lined up or yo' ass gon' stay on maternity leave?" I forced a chuckle through my nose at Cree's remark.

"Oh you got jokes," I replied, putting out the blunt. Reaching over, I opened a window to air out the room after suddenly deciding that I wanted to bring my princess down to watch the game later on with me. Yeah, I know I just said this was my man cave but I made the rules so I could break them every now and then. Especially when it came to my daughter.

"No jokes. Just wanted to know if you was gonna pull a Kane and become a family man. You know... walk the straight and narrow road from now on—" Before he could finish his sentence, Cree erupted into a fit of coughs.

"You can't even get it out because you know it's bullshit. I ain't never retiring from the game and I put that on everything. What would niggas in the hood do if 'Law wasn't around to run shit?"

Cree got himself together and cleared his throat before replying. "Shit, I don't know. Listen, I'm smokin' on some new shit Gunplay just dropped off over here and it's stinging my fuckin' chest. Bruh... I think I'mma need an X-ray."

Frowning, I pulled the phone from my ear and looked at it, wishing I could slap the fuck outta my brother right then.

"Bruh, you tweakin'. I done told you 'bout smokin' alone. You need to stick to Yolo's jungle juice and leave the weed alone. You ain't built to handle that shit."

"How you figure?"

Chuckling, I shook my head, not believin' that Cree really wanted me to explain what we all knew. I didn't even bother replying to him because it would have been a waste of my time. Since the very beginning,

Cree has never been able to smoke out with us unless Yolo cooked him up something to help mellow him out and relax. Otherwise, Cree's ass was liable to get all of our asses arrested.

"Cree! I—I think I see somebody runnin' around in the backyard. We need to call the cops!" I heard a female yelling in the background, in full panic mode, and I knew it was Carmella.

"Mel, put that fuckin' phone down before you get both of us locked the hell up!"

"Damn, bruh, you let her smoke, too? She seein' clowns like you?" I couldn't believe this shit. It was classic and I was damn near about to fall over laughing.

"Man, she buggin' off a contact high. I ain't even let her take a pull!"

I continued to laugh at Cree's expense. It was obvious that he had found the one for him, and as much as I teased him about it, I was honestly happy for him. Carmella was wild and I still thought that he needed to learn how to put a stop to that smart ass mouth she had but she was straight with me.

"Damn, I forgot to tell you, y'all need to come out to the house tomorrow. Since Janelle ain't have no baby shower, she wanted to do a cook out and have everybody over here since our folks in town. Her dad and sisters flyin' in tonight."

"Word? They stayin' there?"

I nodded my head as a smug half-smirk came up on my face. "You muthafuckin' right they are."

When Janelle told me her pops was coming into town to check on her and the baby, I made a point in letting her know that his ass would be staying right here in the house I'd bought her just so I could shine on his ass. When it came to pleasing Janelle, she didn't require much so I could have just got her a lil' regular ass crib and she would have been just as happy. But after seeing the mansion she'd grown up in, I was determined not to be outdone and immediately copped a muthafuckin' estate. I even brought in an interior decorator to make sure this bitch was laced to the max in time for her pops' visit so a hotel was out of the question. I couldn't stunt on his ass properly if he was staying at the Westin.

"That's what's up. I see you, nigga! And I know yo' flashy ass went all out for the occasion. Probably got zebras and fuckin' gazelles runnin' around in the backyard and shit." Cree laughed at his own joke and I bust a few chuckles along with him.

"Just a little bit of razzle dazzle. Regular shit," I told him, rubbing at my beard.

"Bullshit," Cree replied. "Ain't nothin' regular 'bout yo' ass, bruh. I'll expect to be amazed."

***

"Why in the world are you dressed like that? My daddy said he's almost here!"

Walking into our bedroom, Janelle gawked at me like she wasn't sure I hadn't lost my mind but I knew I was fly. Like Biggie Smalls, I was Gucci down to the socks, wearing silk Gucci pajama pants, a silk Gucci shirt and fuzzy Gucci slippers with multiple thick gold chains draped around my neck looking like a gangsta Hugh Hefner. Between my lips was a Cuban cigar and I had one in my stash to give her pops as soon as he pulled up. I was on my grown man shit.

"What you mean?" I asked, crinkling my brows as I looked down at my fit. "I'm fly as hell!"

She widened her eyes and looked me up and down with a doubtful expression on her face.

"You look like you're wearin' our bedroom sheets. What's with all the silk?"

I grabbed my crotch suggestively and shot her an evil smirk. "Niggas love this shit but not everybody can afford it. Feels good on our nuts."

Her mouth dropped open and her eyes bugged even further. "You don't have on boxers?!"

"Fuck yeah! What you think I'm walkin' around with my ass on the loose? What kinda gay ass shit is that? I got on boxers... them shits is silk too!" I peeled down the waist of my pajama pants to demonstrate, showing her how a nigga like me got down. My shirt and pants were navy blue but my boxers and slippers were blood red to match the red-rimmed glasses on my face. You couldn't teach this level of fly.

"You color coordinated your boxers and glasses to match your outfit." Janelle's tone was flat. "This might be a little too much... even for you."

"Don't be a hater all your life," I remarked, eyeing the loose-fitting black dress that she was wearing along with a pair of heels so close to the ground, she might as well have been sporting shower slides. I narrowed my eyes at her and pulled the cigar from my lips, using it to point at her.

"I see God would be pleased with your outfit."

She rolled her eyes and ignored me, placing her hand on her hip. "Where is January?"

Just the question I wanted her to ask. Dropping the cigar onto the small end table next to the bed, I pulled back the covers and grabbed my baby girl into my hands, grinning hard as I showed her off to her mama. Janelle's mouth dropped open in the exact way I'd suspected as soon as she laid eyes on her.

"I can't believe this shit," she mumbled, shaking her head. "You got her an outfit to match you? Where the hell did you find that?!"

Yeah, you read that right! My baby was destined to be a boss and I was going to make sure that she dressed the part. January was stuntin' like her daddy, wearing a baby version of what I had on, except hers was in pink. Since her feet were too tiny for shoes, she had on fuzzy pink Gucci socks.

"You know she cute. Admit it."

Janelle couldn't deny the fact and when I saw the edges of her lips curl up into a smile, I knew I'd won. Reaching her arms out, she went to grab January but I snatched her away.

"Let me hold her, Luke! My daddy should be here by now!"

With my nose screwed up like I smelled something disgusting, I looked at Janelle and shook my head. "I would let you hold her but this is silk and you wearin' cotton. I can't let the two rub together."

"Nigga, if you don't—"

Eyes flashing and attitude on one hundred, Janelle snatched January out of my arms and I almost choked laughing at her crazy ass. It was so easy to get under her skin. She turned to walk away, swishing them sexy hips from side-to-side, and I couldn't resist smacking her hard on her ass.

"When I first saw you in the courthouse wearing that church skirt, I was wonderin' what ya mama gave ya. Now I know."

Biting down on my bottom lip, I squeezed her plump ass between my fingers, enjoying the extra weight that she'd gained from being pregnant. She cut her eyes at me but there was no hiding the smirk on her face. No matter how Janelle acted in public, she couldn't deny that she loved that thug shit.

"Oh God, they are pullin' up in the yard!"

It was about five minutes later and Janelle was trippin' like we had Oprah and Stedman coming to dinner instead of just her father and sisters. Tossing January into my arms, she ran her hand over her hair and pulled at her loose curls before wringing her hands in front of her.

"Yo, chill," I instructed her. "If you need to take a hit, I got some Loud in the—"

She slapped her hand to her chest and dropped her bottom jaw open like she couldn't believe what I was saying. I just shook my head and tried to bite down on the smile that I felt coming. Janelle was hilarious and she didn't even know it.

There was a knock on the door and Janelle counted to five slowly before walking to answer it, as if she hadn't been standing there the whole time in anticipation of that moment. I couldn't deal with her ass. Looking down at my baby girl who was still asleep in my arms, I wondered if she would act more like me or her mother.

"Daddy!" Janelle squealed when she opened the door and jumped up to wrap her arms around her father.

"Hey baby."

Her father's laugh echoed through the room and January began to stir awake. After greeting Janelle, her father's bold and coffee brown eyes fell on me and I stepped up, holding one hand out to shake his as I held January to my chest with the other.

"Luke... nice to see you once again."

I nodded my head and gave his hand a firm shake. "Good to see you too, George. Welcome to our humble abode, it's not much but I hope it's to your liking."

Janelle shot her eyes to me and rolled them dramatically.

"Your *humble* abode, huh?" George repeated with a knowing smirk as he glanced around the foyer, taking in all the décor that I'd spent a grip on.

"Yes, there is so much more that I want to do to the place but we're still settling in," I replied casually, not even bothering to let him know that the area rug he had his dusty boots on had cost fifty grand.

Don't get me wrong, I ain't into impressing niggas. But regardless to how shit was now, I would never forget the moment when George made it clear that he thought I wasn't good enough for his daughter just because I was from the streets. Eventually he got over that and now Janelle was my wife, but I would forever remind George that there wasn't a damn thing in the world a nigga could do for Janelle that I couldn't do better. And that included his ass too.

"This crib is *nice!*" Janelle's youngest sister gushed loudly as soon as she walked through the door, rolling her suitcase behind her.

"It *is* nice…" her sister, Mixie, added when she walked in behind her. "Jani, Luke must've decorated because I know your style and this is not it."

"You're right." Janelle giggled. "Luke got an interior decorator to come in and—"

"Daaaaamn," TreVonia interrupted, her eyes wide as she marveled at the paintings on the wall.

Stopping abruptly, she stood in front of one that held a special place in my heart. I'd stolen it during one of our first hits. Kane had stumbled upon a crazy nigga in the hood, heroin addict who could paint his ass off when he was high, and that's how he came up with the idea for our first major lick. We robbed a museum and replaced a few of the paintings with fakes that he'd had the addict make. No one even knew a crime had occurred because I'd put my skills to the test. Being that it was my first job, it took me weeks to break into their security system. I was much faster now.

"Is this an actual Picasso?!" Mixie asked, adjusting her glasses to squint at the painting TreVonia was in front of.

"Nah, it's a fake," I lied with a shrug.

"A *really* good one," George added, walking up beside his daughters. "I love art and this—this painting is remarkably close to the original. It's hard to believe that it's a replica."

I smiled hard as I watched them, knowing that I looked like the cat that had swallowed the canary. Then I suddenly felt the heat of Janelle's eyes on my face and I turned to her, seeing that she had her piercing eyes on me, narrowed as she questioned me without speaking.

"It's a fake!" I mouthed to her but she twisted her lips up to the side. I knew she ain't believe me.

Handing the baby off to Janelle, I took everyone's luggage to their rooms as they all 'oohed' and 'ahhed' over January and how cute she was. By the time that I came back down, using the elevator instead of the stairs, the women were all huddled together listening to Janelle go over the pains of childbirth and George was walking around the house with his spectacles on his face and his hands clasped behind his back, studying the art on the walls.

"Did the decorator pick out these pieces?" he asked, not looking at me while he scrutinized each work of art individually before moving to the next one.

I nudged my long braid behind my back and shook my head before standing next to him.

"Nah, the art and the statues are all me. I've been collectin' them over the years," I replied with pride.

I had a keepsake in my house from every job that I did with my brothers, no matter how big and no matter how small. When Pelmington was still on our ass, I used to joke that if he ever ran up in my crib, he'd find all kinds of shit related to the jobs we'd pulled off, whether he knew we were behind them or not. Kane thought it was foolish but I didn't give a shit.

Bottom line was even with all the things I'd collected, Pelmington wouldn't ever be able to tie me to the crimes. For all he knew, I could've bought this shit off the street. I was cocky and arrogant but I wasn't stupid.

"I never did get a chance to tell you welcome to the family," George began, still looking at the paintings. "I've always wanted a son. Never got one but I guess a son-in-law is the next best thing."

Never before had I cared about getting the approval of another man, not even when it came to my own father, but I did appreciate George letting me know that he was focused on making peace with me. Might as well because I wasn't going anywhere but I appreciated the effort.

"I'm going to do right by your daughter," I told him with pure honesty. "I may not be the type of man you thought she'd be with but there isn't one out there who is better for her than me."

Without saying anything and still not looking my way, George nodded his head and we stood in silence for a short while, admiring the art on the walls.

"I know these aren't replicas," George said finally and cut his eyes to look at me. "I would ask you how it is that they are here when they should be in various museums in France, Italy and Rome but I think I'll leave that question alone for now."

Clearing my throat, I tried to hide my smirk. Janelle's pops was no fool and we both knew it. He'd done his research on me and I was sure he knew what my brothers and I were capable of.

"You and I both chose different paths for our lives, not to say one is better than the other," he clarified quickly. "But they are different to say the least. And the one you chose is dangerous and involves more risk."

He turned to me, watching my face with intensity as I stood silently. I knew there was a lot he felt he needed to say and I was going to give him the space to say it. Having a daughter now, I could understand how it was in his shoes, worried that his daughter might be linked with a nigga who could either make her a widow or an accomplice to a major crime.

"I just want to be sure that my daughter and grand-daughter are able to live a safe and happy life." He pushed the glasses up on his face, making me think of how Janelle did the same exact thing. "You do take proper precautions, right? I mean—when it comes to what you do… you plan everything out, right? Making sure to pay attention to every little detail?"

With a straight face, I stood firmly in front of him and stared back, not saying a word. It didn't matter if he was Janelle's father or not, when it came to the things I did with my brothers, I didn't speak on it.

Realizing that he wasn't about to get the response that he wanted, he sighed heavily and let his head hang. I could see the weariness and distress all over his face.

"When it comes to my family, I do everything in my power to make sure they are happy as well as safe. Never will I give anyone a reason to question that."

It was the only reassurance I could give him but it seemed to be just enough for George. Standing up tall, he nodded his head and reached out to give me a firm pat on the back.

"I trust you won't."

Feeling like I was being watched, I waited until George's attention went back to the artwork before I turned and glanced back down the hall. My eyes connected instantly with Janelle's and the expression of admiration and love that was in them warmed my whole body in the way that only she could.

"I love you," she mouthed to me and I responded by patting my chest, right above my heart.

She seemed to blush, bending her head slightly as then she smiled. I watched her carefully, taking a mental photograph of what I was seeing in front of me. The image of my wife, best friend and love of my life, holding my baby girl in her arms was something that I would hold on to and think of every time I made a move in the streets. They were my life, my entire world, and I knew there was no way I could live a day on this Earth without them. They would be the sole reason that, no matter what I was caught up in, I would always make it back home.

Janelle

*L*ife couldn't get any better than it was *right* now. And I probably said that a million times a day but *this* time, I meant it.

"Jani, are you done feeding her already?! I wanna hold her!" TreVonia huffed, peeking down at January as I cradled her in my arms. "I think you like breastfeeding that lil' girl more than she do!"

"It's our bonding time," I informed TreVonia and she simply rolled her eyes. "Fine, I'll burp her really quickly and then you can have her."

It was somewhat of a compromise because January was already done feeding so I had no other choice anyways. Still, TreVonia seemed to be in agreement, her face brightening up as she nodded her head.

"Okay, I'm going to grab a hotdog really quick and then I'll be back. Tank know he can grill up some food! You tried any of it yet, Mixie?"

Rolling her eyes, Mixie crossed her arms in front of her chest. "I'm vegan."

"Girl, bye! Since when?"

I waited along with TreVonia for her response but she didn't say a word and simply shot her eyes over to Tank before turning up her nose and looking away. There was nothing left to say because I could read it all in her expression. She was a vegan only because Tank was the one cooking the meat.

"You need to stop sulking and pouting just because he brought a girl out here with him. Anyone with eyes knows that he ain't even feelin' that broad. He just brought her here to teach you a lesson," TreVonia reasoned and I had to agree.

For the past few months, Tank had been trying to convince Mixie to be his girlfriend and make things official but Mixie rejected the idea each time, stating that she didn't like labels. Sometimes I thought that Mixie's genius was a gift and a curse. She was one of those people who considered herself 'woke' so she fought against anything that she deemed as 'the system'. She couldn't be Tank's girlfriend because she thought it was just another way that men staked their claim on women, treating them more as property than real people with brains and feelings.

All that shit flipped on her when Tank showed up to the barbecue with another woman on his arm. When Luke asked him who she was, Tank made sure that Mixie was within earshot and loudly proclaimed that he wouldn't be able to say what the woman was to him because he wasn't a fan of labels but her name was Patrice and he was currently enjoying her company. Mixie had an attitude ever since.

"That's the problem with men these days," Mixie began, sticking her nose high in the air. "They think they have to teach us lessons. We are their equals! I refuse to allow someone to think he can train me like a dog. Do you think that Angela Davis—"

Shaking my head, I only half-listened as Mixie crooned on like the president of the NAACW: The National Association for the

Advancement of Black Women. As much as she didn't want to admit it, she was feeling Tank and how she was acting was only proof of it. He'd done exactly what he aimed to do when he showed up with another woman, knowing that Mixie was in town. When it came to the Murrays, they didn't fight fair and the quicker Mixie realized that, the easier it would be for her.

At any rate, besides Mixie's relationship issues, the barbecue was going perfectly. My daddy was getting along with Luke's father as if they were old friends. They had so much in common that it was almost funny. Tayesha had flown in that morning and she fit right in with Luke's mother and grandmother. She and my daddy hadn't announced their relationship yet but it was obvious to anyone watching their interaction that they had strong feelings for each other.

"What's up, Janelle? Can I sit here?" Sidney asked but didn't wait before she plopped her butt right down in the chair next to me. Pulling her leg up on the seat, she tied up the laces on one sneaker before doing the other and then scooping her long hair up into a high ponytail.

"You straightened your hair… it looks nice." I smiled, noticing that even though Sidney tried to act like it was nothing, she was beaming at the compliment.

"Thanks. Teema did it for me."

"What are you about to do?!" a voice to the side of us snapped.

"Speaking of the devil," Sidney scoffed just as Teema walked up. She stood in front of Sidney with her hands on her hips and her eyes narrowed. Sidney held her hands out, palms up.

"What it look like? I'm about to play basketball with the boys!"

Smacking her lips, Teema rolled her eyes and sighed heavily before flopping down in the chair next to Sidney.

"How many times I gotta tell you that you can't be sweatin' and shit after I flatiron your hair! You are not one of the boys! It won't hurt you to sit your tail down and just watch the game for once in your life!"

Jumping up, Sidney wrinkled up her nose and stuck her tongue out at Teema before grinning and running away to where Yolo was standing, waiting on her. He wrapped his arm around her shoulder and kissed her on the cheek as they walked to the basketball court that Luke had installed in our backyard. Luke, Kane, Tank and Cree were already over there waiting.

"I think y'all should make room for another man," Luke's dad shouted, standing up. Before anyone could respond to him, he unbuttoned his polo shirt and pulled it off, showing off the Lebron James jersey he had on underneath. Reaching into his pocket, he pulled out a headband and pushed it down over his head, grinning mischievously while his sons watched.

"Aw, hell naw!" Luke yelled. "We got money on this game. We ain't got room for you, old school."

"You know what?" I heard my own daddy say, to my utter surprise. "I think I wanna play, too."

"Hell naw," Luke shouted once more. "Kane is the ref for the first game. That's too many men on one team."

Not missing a beat, Teema jumped up with a quick solution. "Sid's ass can sit this one out then. She don't need to be out there anyways!"

With her lips poked out, Sidney crossed her arms and kissed Yolo before jogging off the court, giving up her spot. She sat down next to Teema and pressed her middle finger against Teema's nose, right between her eyes. I giggled as Teema knocked it away while cursing Sidney out for being so disrespectful.

"Where is Carmella?"

No sooner than I'd asked the question, Carmella walked out of the house with Bryan by her side, both of them wearing cheerleading uniforms. While Carmella donned a pleated skirt and a cute top, Bryan wore track pants and a white t-shirt with a matching headband. Both of them had pom-poms in their hands, waving them high above their heads. Everyone burst out laughing and Bryan squealed before throwing his leg up to do a toe-touch.

"That nigga just stretched his whole leg up in the fuckin' air. This some bullshit," I heard Luke say, shaking his head incredulously but even he couldn't help but laugh at Bryan's antics.

Cree ran over to the sound system we had set up and crank the music up to really get the party started. Tank's kids all jumped up to dance and Yolo's son was right behind them, happily flailing his limbs in the air to the beat. He made a miss-step and tripped over his own foot, tumbling forward before he landed with a *thump*, flat on his back. With a high-pitched squawk, Sidney leaped up into the air like her ass was on fire and ran over to help him up, dusting the dirt off his butt.

"Jeremiah! Are you okay?!"

Seeing the concern in Sidney's face, Jeremiah dropped his body lip, allowing it to tremble.

"Yeah, his ass is okay! Sid, sit'cho worrisome ass down and let that lil' nigga be a man!" Luke yelled with his brothers standing by his side, nodding their heads in agreement.

"He's not a man, he's a baby!" she protested, waving Luke off with her hand.

"And he gon' stay a baby if you keep kissin' his boo-boos. Chill and let my man do what he do. He ain't soft!" Yolo added and Sidney reluctantly listened, letting Jeremiah go. As soon as he was free, he was back to playing and dancing with his cousins.

"I just think it's so stupid the way that when little boys fall, they get tough love because they need to be a man and to baby them supposedly makes them weak. But when a little girl falls, she's babied and it's acceptable! Does that mean it's acceptable for her to be weak?" Mixie chimed in searching around the table for someone to give her an answer to her question. When no one said a word, she continued.

"I mean, why is January any different from Jeremiah? She can't be strong, too?"

Laughing, I held my baby up and gave her a kiss on the cheek. With each day, she was growing more and more into her features but I still was on the fence about who she looked like. It seemed like she was the perfect blend of me and Luke. She had his thick, silky jet-black hair, my rich chocolate brown complexion and his intense, fiery eyes. She was like a little chocolate china doll, so beautiful in every way. Just perfect.

"She has no choice but to be strong. You know who her parents are?"

Scoffing, Mixie rolled her eyes and went back to a book that she had told us was just for some 'light reading': *The Destruction of Black Civilization* by Chancellor Williams. As soon as she lifted it up to her face, Tank slam-dunked the basketball into the goal and everybody cheered loudly.

"That shot right there was for you, Mixie!" He roared to the top of his lungs, pointing at Mixie as his brothers all amped him up. "I did that for you, girl! Come over here and give me a fat, sloppy kiss for good luck!"

Peeking at him from over the rim of her glasses, Mixie twisted her lips up and let out an indignant snort but when she bent her head down into her book, I saw her hiding a smile behind the pages. She definitely wanted Tank. She wasn't fooling anyone but herself.

Once the game ended, Yolo pulled out the cards and dominos and I took the opportunity to run to the bathroom while Luke's grandmother was rocking January to sleep. I was washing my hands when the door opened and Luke rushed in, closing and locking it behind him.

"What are you up to?" I asked, smiling at the devilish grin on his face.

With one brow lifted, he looked me over and licked his lips suggestively. My eyes widened to enormous proportions and I backed away, shaking my head as I pressed my palms flat against his chest.

"I can't! You know the doctor said we gotta wait six weeks!"

"Black chicks got that snap-back so y'all ain't gotta wait that long." He actually said that line with a straight ass face and an authoritative tone, like it was the truth. Leaning over, Luke reached for me and I slapped his hands away.

"That ain't true! I gotta wait six weeks just like everybody else."

He cocked his head to the side and narrowed his eyes like he couldn't believe I didn't know something he knew.

"It *is* true. Black chicks got melanin in y'all skin so you heal faster. For real! Chicks in the hood be fuckin' the same damn week they get back from the hospital. Some of them be pregnant before their 6-week checkup. It's a fact."

I giggled, not believing that he was actually trying to convince me of something I knew damn well was not true. The crazy part of it was that he was so smooth with it, he actually had me thinking about it!

"I'm not having sex with you, Luke, so you can stop it," I told him. "But if you play your cards right, you might get some head tonight."

Teasing him, I bit down on my bottom lip sexily and then licked them slowly, watching as his eyes trailed my tongue.

"Deal." He smacked me hard on my backside and gave it a tight squeeze before letting himself out of the bathroom and shutting the door.

Laughing to myself, I went back to the mirror to check my hair and clothes, making sure that I was straight after dealing with Luke and his insanity. Once I was satisfied that my appearance was on point, I went back outside to laugh, talk and have fun with my family... my *entire* family. We were probably the most unlikely crew to ever be in a single place together: mastermind criminals mixed in with ivy league educated attorneys, socialites, Black political enthusiasts and a retired kingpin. Who could've come up with that? But we were the perfect mix of people who loved and accepted each other—that was the common link that bound us all.

Life couldn't get any better than it was *right* now. And this time, I meant it. Really!

THE END!

NOTE FROM PORSCHA STERLING

Thank you for reading!

I wasn't planning on writing book number FIVE but after looking at the reviews for book 4, I saw many requests for more and a lot of readers saying that these characters' stories seemed incomplete. Based on that, I decided to wrap up a few things in this installment of the Bad Boys series. BUT I've also had a few requests for more on the other Murray brothers, including a book on Mixie and Tank—let me know in the reviews if you want it and I'll consider it!

I hope you enjoyed reading about Outlaw, his brothers and the women they loved. I'm definitely going to miss the entire crew. It's hard to say goodbye.

Join my Facebook group (Porscha Sterling's VIP Reading Group) so you can get some exclusives and interact with me. I love to hear what you all have to say! I love to interact with my readers because I APPRECIATE ALL OF YOU! Hit me up!

Check out my website to get an overview of the characters mentioned in this installment of the series. I pulled some visuals so you'll know what they kind of look like to me when I'm writing about them. Hope you like what you see! Visit www.porschasterling.com to check them out!

Please make sure to leave a review! I love reading them!

I would love it if you reach out to me on Facebook, Instagram or Twitter!

If you haven't already, text PORSCHA to 25827 to join my text list. Text ROYALTY to 42828 to join our email list and read excerpts and learn about giveaways.

Peace, love & blessings to everyone. I love allllll of you!

Porscha Sterling

MAKE SURE TO LEAVE A REVIEW!

Text PORSCHA to 25827
to keep up with Porscha's latest releases!

To find out more about her, visit www.porschasterling.com

Join our mailing list to get a notification when Leo Sullivan Presents has another release! Text **LEOSULLIVAN** to **22828** to join!

To submit a manuscript for our review, email us at leosullivanpresents@gmail.com

Get LiT!

Download the LiT app today and enjoy exclusive content, free books, and more!

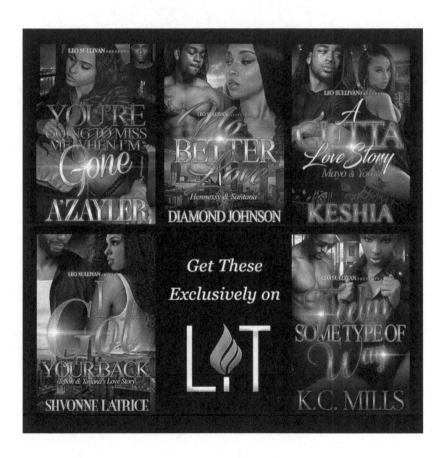

DEC 0 3 2019

CPSIA information can be obtained
at www.ICGtesting.com
Printed in the USA
LVHW040015010319
609156LV00003B/213

9 781946 789082